'A dark   eets

of Victorian Cardiff. I loved it!'

From Crawll Letters from the Lighthouse

Knowsley Council

Knowsley Library Service

Please return this book on or
before the date shown below

GASLIGHT

Eloise Williams

Firefly

First published in 2017
by Firefly Press
25 Gabalfa Road, Llandaff North, Cardiff, CF14 2JJ
www.fireflypress.co.uk

A CIP catalogue record of this book is available from
the British Library.

1 3 5 7 9 8 6 4 2

print ISBN: 9781910080542
ebook ISBN 9781910080559

This book has been published with the support of the
Welsh Books Council.

Chapter heading illustrations © Guy Manning
Typeset by: Elaine Sharples

Printed and bound by CPI Group UK

To (Arthur) Warren Howe, an old style Cardiff kid. Gone sailing.

Rosie Marina, an all-new Cardiff kid. Jeans rolled up to the knee, paddling.

Prologue

My mother disappeared on the sixth of September, 1894.

I was found at the docks in Cardiff, lying like a gutted fish at the water's edge.

I was found at first light. I was half drowned. No one reported me missing and no paper covered my story, though I coined the name 'The Mysterious Mermaid' when I told the tale. I don't know how I got there. I don't know what happened to my mother. People say perhaps I got a bump on the head, giving me memory loss, or perhaps something so traumatic happened to me that I've blocked it out. I don't care what happened to me. I only care what happened to her.

She had red hair like mine but brighter, glossy and thick, and so long you could plait it down her back when she let it loose. She had the face of an angel and eyes of such a deep navy you could swim in them. Her height (I'm guessing here) was five feet five. Her distinguishing features were: freckles on her lower lip, dimples when she smiled, a birthmark on her wrist in the shape of a crescent moon. When she went missing she had a black eye and her left arm in a sling. I can remember her in that moment so clearly. But everything else is darkness.

We were running from my father. Sid told me. I was so lucky Sid was kind enough to take me in. We were running because women don't leave their husbands without going to the workhouse and if he caught us he would kill us, or commit us to the asylum. We were running – that's the last thing I remember. That and the rolling darkness.

It's the not knowing. The echoing not knowing. As dawn breaks. In the midday sun. As the night catches us in sleep.

Have you seen her?

1

Cardiff, August 1899

I'm drowning. I'm floating.

I'm drowning. I'm floating.

I'm drowning.

Even though I'm fourteen I already understand that life is complicated. I have to remember who I am, for a start.

When I'm thieving I'm Tilly Thomas. The darkest shadow. Ducking and diving. Filching and stealing. Wanting to be as invisible as a ghost. Trying to be as unnoticeable as a servant should be.

When I'm on stage I'm Ruby Radclyffe. Twinkling as the brightest light. Vibrant and jolly with my lips painted pillar-box red and my body filled with charisma like a hot air balloon. Shining and spinning like the star I'm going to be.

When I'm Nansi Howells, I am really me.

Like now: I'm swimming in the lake. Drowning. Floating. Naked. Studying the night sky. Wondering what lies beneath the water.

Fallen chimney sweeps who have turned into water babies? Unlikely.

A hungry giant water serpent with huge fangs and the ability to chew through my bones in seconds? Also unlikely, but it makes me splash a bit.

When I settle again, it hits me how strange it is that here I can choose between sinking or living. I think of myself as a mermaid. A water nymph. Something other. Ears filled with the thrum of the lake and limbs slapping the water like gentle fins. Of course, having to keep half an eye on the place where I left my clothes brings me back down to earth. It's a risk. People will nick anything they can get their hands on and I don't really want to be scarpering across Cardiff in the altogether. I can't say I would blame them for stealing from me. I'm not pure as the driven snow myself, am I?

Tonight has been a terrible night. One of the worst so far. But there's no arguing with Sid when he wants something done and he's threatening the gallows. The water will help with the bruise on my arm. It'll wash off the blood where that monster ripped the hair from my scalp. It'll help to clean the fear away.

I take a deep breath and float with my ears under the surface. The back of my head throbs. The cold beats at my eardrums, but if I concentrate I can get past the pain. I stare at the sky and swim out the filth of the day. The girl's face when she woke to find me in her bedroom. That evil man's shouts. I ignore the rattle and scruff and blood of Cardiff and let the lap of the water at my belly drink me down. I try to think of nothing else.

I don't think about my mother.

I don't imagine her soft hands and her musical laugh.

I don't think about us walking together through the woods. Picking bluebells together. Drinking hot cocoa in front of an open fire.

I don't wonder why she disappeared and left me here. I don't wonder if she is watching over me from somewhere far away. From the tip of a twinkling star perhaps. Swinging from the crook of the moon.

I shudder and tell myself sternly that she is alive. She is alive.

I try to think about all the details of her face to make me feel better, but even though I don't want to, I imagine myself in the theatre instead, and the audience are booing and hissing at me. Sid is there, smirking at the side of the stage. He taps his cane on the boards as if he is conducting them. The smoke is hazy in the heat and the burning lime of the footlights scorches the air. There's a song playing but it's not one I recognise. It's getting slower and slower as I sink. The audience stop their jeering and gaze fixedly as I disappear into the water, as if I never really existed. Sucked up by the mirror of the starry sky. A girl from a fairy tale who was never real at all.

My mother's face comes into focus and she calls out 'Ruby' to try to save me. It's not my real name.

I come up for air as dawn breaks. It's hard to drown when you are as good at swimming as I am.

2

'Oi! Watch it!' He's a fully grown man but he almost topples as I run into him.

'Sorry, sorry, sorry.' I'm not really sorry. I'm in too much of a rush to feel anything. The ridiculousness of almost knocking over one of the knocker-uppers doesn't escape me. It'll make a funny story for the others. But I think I freaked the poor bloke out, pegging it along here, soaking wet through though there's been no rain. People are always on their guard against lunatics and rogues in the early hours. Myself included. That's one of the reasons I was running in the first place.

'Bloody kids!'

'I said I'm sorry.' I stop, to help him up from where I've bowled him over in the horse dung, but he takes a swipe at me with his hammy hands, so I start running again. He's been annoying people since before dawn by charging them money to get them out of bed, so I tell myself I got some revenge for them.

My breath comes in sharp white blasts by the time I get to the Empire and I have to bend over and stand with my hands on my knees to get rid of the stitch that's pranging my ribs. My skirts are stinking up as far as my shins. I can't begin to imagine what I must look like. Awful, that's for sure. I try to tidy my hair but it's too scratty and tangled. It's dripped right through my dress. Even though this early autumn has been warm, it's freezing this morning and I'm shivering. Being this tired all the time doesn't help. I stand in a haberdasher's shop doorway and peek at the outside of the theatre, to check that Sid isn't about. Of course he isn't. No one is. They aren't early risers, this lot. They are late night partiers or have a second way to earn some pennies that takes them through to the first grey hours of dawn.

I let myself in. Sid's good like that at least. He's given me a room of my own in the backstage cellars and I have a mattress to myself, so I can't complain. The room is practically a box and has an odour that is indescribable. But it's better than nothing and it's mine. I've put some flowers in a jar on the trunk in the corner and they help to brighten the darkness with the orange and lilac sway of their heads. Their smell is too fragile to battle the stench but I'm grateful for it anyway. It reminds me of the heavy scents of summer: lilacs, peonies, marigolds, peppery sweet on the air.

My real clothes are hung up next to some old, moth-eaten costumes, so I get out of this servant's uniform, part of Sid's latest cunning plan, and try to shake the cold out of them before putting them on. It doesn't work. Even in the middle of summer it's an ice pit down here. I light an oil lamp and try to appreciate the vague sense of heat.

My reflection, when I get up the courage to look at it, is ghastly. My hair, which is just the wrong sort of red, is still dirty even though it's wet and looks like a swan's nest. I need to try to sort myself out pretty quickly so I can get some kip before Sid wants me, wants to see the spoils of last night (not that I have any) and give me my work for today.

A shiver convulses my body as I think of that girl again. I should've tried to convince her that I was a real servant like I'm supposed to, but I was so afraid I just froze to the spot, staring at her like a startled hare. She probably thought I was a ghost. Or some kind of madhouse escapee.

'Sid won't be pleased,' I tell the girl in the glass, who is wincing as she rubs the bald patch on her head. 'If he finds out.'

It all happened so fast. I hid in the girl's wardrobe when the other servants went to bed. I came out when I was sure it was dark and everyone was asleep, to go downstairs and rifle through their silver, as I'd been ordered. And then I saw it. A book. So beautiful. I thought it would be such a gorgeous thing for Bee to have. I've been trying to teach her to read, in minutes snatched from our real jobs, and it was so tempting to have a real book to learn from instead of just Penny Dreadfuls. It was lying there waiting in the darkness. 'Notice me. Look at me,' it whispered, the gold lettering catching the light on the crimson cover, the gilt-edged pages glittering. 'I promise you wonderful stories.' It was waiting there just for me.

I knew it was a risk to go so close to the sleeping girl but I couldn't get Bee's excited face out of my head. So I went for it. As I reached out the floorboards creaked, the way things always make a racket when you are trying to be quiet.

'Who's there?' The girl sprang up in her bed like a jumping jack-in-the-box and I just stood, a petrified tailor's dummy, with the book in my hand, and my mouth open to catch flies.

She gawped at me.

I gawped back at her.

And then chaos erupted.

'AARRRRRRRGGGGGGGGGGGGHHHHHH HHHHH.' The scream coming out of that tiny mite's mouth could've sunk a ship, I'm telling you. It shocked me into moving.

I ran out of the room and on to the landing, but the house was already waking in confusion. Harassed yelps filled the darkness and lamps were lit. I, of course, had to wait for a second too long to see if my mother was one of the people emerging from the rooms.

'Get the rifle!' someone shouted.

'Burglars.' Someone else.

'Murderers!' An over-dramatic reaction, I thought.

I ran back into the bedroom, making the girl screech louder. I shoved the book in my apron pocket and tried to yank open the window so I could get out. You wouldn't believe how much time it takes to shove one of them sash windows up when your palms are sweating and you're trembling with panic. I was through it, quick as I could, but I held on to the sill, dangling over the garden below. I wasted precious moments praying I wouldn't break my ankle or worse, then this livid man stuck his head out and looked down at me yelling, 'When I get my hands on you I'm going to slit your throat.'

Before I could let myself fall, he grabbed hold of the back of my hair, thunked the front of my head against the wall, and held me there, spitting and snarling like some rabid dog. That's when the screaming really got going from all sides.

'Let go of me!' Me, clamouring, in fear of my very life.

'ARGHHHH!' The girl wailing, I suppose in fear of hers.

'Come here you little…' The man tugging at my hair.

'Call for the police.' 'Is anyone hurt?' 'Did they take my jewels?' 'Shoot on sight and that's an order.' The entire population of the household.

I wailed the loudest and scratched at him like a circus tiger with all my will and might. I think I hurt him because he suddenly swore loudly and dropped me like a stone. I'm lucky to be alive; the landing winded me so badly.

Back in my room, I examine my wounds and see that the bruises and cuts on my legs are ripening already. My lip has been split open. There is a large bald blooded patch on the back of my head which I can see if I use two looking-glasses. Luckily the front of my head only has a small cut where it hit the bricks. It isn't much of a plus but at least I can cover everything else up. I always wait too long. Just in case. It's a mistake I have to make.

I address myself sternly in the glass. 'You do these jobs to make money, Nansi, my girl, so buck up. You and Sid have a deal. When you've saved up enough you can hire a real detective.'

I know Sherlock Holmes is a made-up creation but he would be ideal. People are always talking about him and how he deduces things.

'Your mother is out there and you are going to find her.' If that includes cheating and swindling then that's the way it has got to be. There's always the chance she'll be in one of these houses I get sent to. Perhaps she was also hit on the head and has memory loss. I imagine her catching sight of me and all her wonderful memories coming back. We will go somewhere else and live together. Another city perhaps, in another country. Maybe she already has a house of her own and a room that she has made beautiful for a reason she can't quite put her finger on. I will track her down. No matter what.

'Nansi!' Bee always manages to sneak in without me noticing. It's a talent she has. We've become really good friends since Sid took me in. When I find my mother I'm certain that Bee will come and live with us.

'It's fine, Bee. It's just a graze.' The gape of her mouth tells me it looks worse than I'd hoped but I think I can pin my hair over it. 'You alright?'

She nods even though she looks dog tired. Bee doesn't sleep well here. She has nightmares every night. She has been here so long she doesn't know it can be different. 'Suspicious Sid wants you already. He's in a right one.'

The others call him Pernicious Sid cos he's such a nasty piece of work but Bee always gets it wrong.

I think she does it on purpose to make me laugh. I can't call him that. He's always done his best for me, even if his best is never quite enough.

'I got this for you.'

Her surprise when she sees the book is worth every bit of pain and fright. I hold it out to her and think of a china-blue bedroom, a patterned quilt, a doll's house with a family of tiny dolls. I don't know why.

'Thanks, Nan.' She leafs through it and then closes it and reads the title slowly. 'Grimms. *A book of Fairy Tales*. Sounds grim.'

I laugh. 'We can keep it safe in here if you like?'

We put it in the trunk with my other belongings. A spare dress, a blanket, some bergamot soap that I nicked.

'Tell Sid I'll be up in a minute.' I glance at my reflection again and baulk. 'And Bee, take your time with the message.'

'Will do.' The dark circles under her cinnamon eyes are deep as wells today. She works so hard to keep her place here. As an orphan, she says she is grateful for a roof over her head and a chance to earn her keep. When I'm a star, I'll buy everything for her.

If Sid is in this early, then something is definitely afoot. I would drag a brush through my hair but my head aches and the lake has made my curls spring into life so I'd just make it frizzy. I pin it up as speedily as I can with torn fingernails. It covers the patch but means that I have a less than fashionable clump at the back of my head. I just mop at the blood with the mobcap I'd been wearing for the robbery, and squeeze a straw hat down over it. I put greasepaint over the cut on my forehead, which stings but covers the gash pretty well. My white gloves are stained at the tips but will have to do. Sid isn't good at waiting.

The passages up to Sid's office aren't lit this early in the morning but I'd know my way in the dark. There's quite a few people asleep at the bottom of the stairs, as there always are, and the smell of beer and more disgusting reeks is an inescapable yellow cloud. Gassy Jack is face down on the bottom steps, living up to his name. He was supposed to be there to help me out last night if anything went wrong, but he must've scarpered and come straight back here. I give him a sharp kick as I go past. He groans, rolls over and then nestles down again. His snoring drops an octave.

Every passage in this place has a memory but I can't think about them now. On a clear day I might remember the acts I've laughed with in these rooms. I might think about the midnight parties and the early morning heart-to-hearts. I might be swept away, thinking of the stories I've been regaled with and the brilliance, dazzle and glamour of the world outside these walls that I've yet to see myself.

I could think about when Wally the clown bet that he could tell us more than thirty jokes in less than two minutes and I laughed so hard that beer came through my nose. Or the party which ended up with us planning to put a zoo in Victoria Park and we tried to think of names for the animals and fell about laughing at calling a seal Billy. Billy from the Box Office has never lived it down.

Today I just think about Sid's room and what awaits me there. No laughing matter at all.

However slow and steady I make my steps, I still arrive at his office before I want to. I touch my hat to check the blood hasn't seeped through. There are no new marks on the gloves, so as far as I can tell it's fine. It still hurts like hell though.

I rap on the door, making my knuckles smart.

There's the tiniest hope that Sid will have been called away on urgent business, like the death of a loved one or a medical emergency, and I wait on tenterhooks. Sid always makes people wait. It's a power thing for him. There are rumours that one of the orchestra grew a beard while he waited. It's such a long time I'm actually thinking that my wish has been granted and Sid is temporarily dead. I wouldn't wish him really dead. He isn't all that bad.

'Entrez.'

Damn. I straighten the hat again and put on my best calm face. I've learned how to act here.

'Ah, the lovely Nansi. Or would we prefer to be called Ruby today?' He arches one of his eyebrows and I pretend to smile. Sid knows that my worst hate is to be mocked. One day I will be a star and then he'll rue the day.

It's bright in here. It figures that Sid would keep all the light to himself.

'Or perhaps we are hoping to be Tilly?'

An atmosphere blows like the north wind through the room. I swear the gaslight flickers.

'Because rumour has it that Tilly … Thomas, is it?' He looks at me for affirmation. I keep my smile so fixed I feel as if rigor mortis has set in. I can taste a mixture of sweat, lake and fear on my lips.

He looks away. 'Yes, Tilly Thomas was apparently seen by a member of the public last night.'

He is so still, I think perhaps the atmosphere has frozen him solid. I listen to the creak of the floorboards expanding in the heat of the fire. I listen to my heart moving up through my body and trying to leave through my rictus grin mouth.

Finally he moves, pushing the nib of his pen into the desk until it bends and splatters ink everywhere.

'I...' My voice falters. I can usually think of something to say, but I've never been nearly caught before. It's almost worse than actually being caught and taken to the workhouse or jail.

'Don't be afraid, Nansi. I'm not angry. For the moment. I'm disappointed. Very disappointed.'

This is worse than if he was angry. Not because I feel guilty that he is disappointed in me, but because there will be something cruel attached to this disappointment. For all that Sid has done for me, I've seen him use things against people and it's not a pretty sight.

'You see if Tilly Thomas is seen and recognised, then it might well lead the police to come here…' Everyone is afraid of the rozzers, even Sid. 'That wouldn't do at all, now, would it?'

I recover my voice, though it sounds like someone else's. 'It wasn't that bad, Sid. He only got a quick peek at my face and I didn't manage to steal anything. I know he wouldn't recognise me again from what he saw. I…'

Sid is around the desk with his hands tight around my throat, quicker than a theatre rat up a stage rope.

'Don't lie to me. He had you dangling from the window like a puppet on a string. Don't tell me he didn't see you or I'll kill you, understand? I don't like lies, Nansi. Understand?'

I feel venomous spit land all over my face with every word. I try to speak, but he's strangling me and nothing comes out but a sharp pin of air. I try to nod but my head is locked in his grip and I can't. Sid's eyes are so close to mine I can see flecks of gold in them like tiny stabbing swords. I'm going to die. The pain is excruciating. There's a lightness in my head and a buzzing sound fills the air like beating wings. I start thinking that the next time I will see my mother again will be never.

Sid loosens his grip slightly and I gulp the cold air deep down into my bones.

He licks the length of my face from my jaw, across my cheek, to my temple. I feel vomit rise in my throat and swallow hard. He is foul.

'Apologies, Nansi.' He lets me go and turns back. My legs give way and I slide down the wall till I'm crumpled on the floor. I watch my hat fall off and spin like a sixpence round and round in circles.

'Lies make me a little irate. After all I've done for you, I'd expect something more. Loyalty perhaps. Honesty certainly.' He is composed again and when he turns he has resumed his jovial expression. 'There, there, Nansi. You know I only have your best interests at heart.'

I force a nod. It's what is expected. Every nerve in my head jangles. I can't even try to smile anymore.

'Good girl.' He smooths his hair back, his hand shiny with oil. 'However, your bad behaviour means you have a bit of making up to do.'

He sits back at the desk as if we are having a

happy chat over afternoon tea and a pastel-pink iced bun. 'Quite a lot of making up to do actually.'

I wait.

'Firstly, we have a new magician arriving.'

I wait, as the fire sparks and dances.

'He will be staying in some digs in Temperance Town.'

I wait, as the gas jets hiss.

'But he has an assistant who needs somewhere to stay so I thought she could share your room.'

And there it is.

'Be a nice bit of company for you, eh? Young girls together. She might even tell you how you can become a star of the stage.' He laughs at his spiteful joke. 'Let her have your bed, Nansi, there's a darling, and you use the floor.'

There is no point in complaining. Sid is one of those people who, if you whinge, gives you a worse reason to protest. After last night, he might kick me out on the streets.

The feeling in my legs is coming back painfully. The numbness rushing into pins and needles.

'Secondly, there is a woman coming here who needs an assistant of her very own.' His eyes gleam. 'She is quite the catch on the European

Market, I'm told, so we are extremely honoured to have her here. Do you understand?'

I wish he'd stop asking if I understand things. Nodding hurts. I nod anyway and bear the brunt of it.

'She has quite an unusual act. I think you'll like it.'

This rouses my interest, in spite of my being almost dead. I am nothing if not ambitious. Perhaps this will finally give me an opportunity to show off my real talents. 'What's the act?'

I mean 'What's my role?' but I won't give him the satisfaction of asking.

'Something to do with dead people.' He flicks an invisible nothing from his trousers.

I'm disappointed that it's just another boring séance act, but I don't want to show it, so I keep my expression stony.

'And no, it's not just another medium act, before you start blubbing. I've had enough of those batty old women, shaking their tambourines and trying to convince everyone that a girl in a white dress is a ghost from the other side. It's far more spectacular. Though it does contain the dead as part of it. Sign of our times, I'm afraid. Everybody's dying and everyone wants a part of it. It's all black hats and feathers, eh?'

I try to look indifferent but slump on the inside. No doubt this woman's act is a séance with a jolly little ditty attached or something. I'll be a ghost girl again, but with a song this time. Hardly the fame and fortune I was hoping for.

'If only there was another life, eh, Nansi?' Even though he isn't even making eye contact, I know he wants me to say something by the tone of his voice.

'I think I've done alright, Sid.' And it is kind of true. It could have been much worse. There are hundreds out there sleeping rough, scrabbling down the mines in the hopeless dark. Sid treats me better than most. I should think myself lucky.

'With me as a father?' He twinkles. He can look almost kind when he wants to.

'With you as a father.'

'I'm so glad we have such strong feelings for each other. I'd hate to think that you might ever say anything about me behind my back.' He picks up a portrait from his desk.

'Course I wouldn't, Sid.'

'This is a likeness of my dear, departed mother.'

He turns the portrait so I can see a stern-looking woman in a dark high-collared gown. 'Had to put her into the asylum for making up tales about me. Terrible shame to put such a smear on my fine character, don't you agree?'

I nod. The workhouse is bad enough. Women burning themselves on irons and steam, forced to work long hours for very little pay, and all of them dropping with hunger and illness. I can't imagine how bad the asylum must be. Or rather I can imagine it, but I don't want to.

'I don't like it when people let me down.' For a moment he looks as if he might weep. I swear I catch a glimpse of genuine sadness in his expression. As if he really had loved her and put her there against his will. Unspeakable things happen at the madhouse.

'I'd simply hate to have to put anyone else there.'

Even an idiot would get this threat.

'The magician's assistant, I forget her name, arrives this afternoon. And Violet Night arrives tomorrow, so be ready to get to work. It's quite the coup to get Ms Night but then I am at the top of the tree.' He grins, dismissing me.

I use every ounce of energy to push myself up

to a standing position. I got off fairly lightly, I suppose. There is a streak of blood down the wall from where Sid held me against it and I can feel the gunky warmth of more blood congealing on my neck. I pick up my hat and put it on at a jaunty angle in defiance.

'Do I have enough saved to hire a detective yet, Sid?'

He lets the question hang between us for a moment, and then a moment more.

'Not yet. But I'll make some enquiries.'

You would think my heart would soar at this, but he has been feeding me the same line for as long as I can recall. I need to push him and ask him to put me in charge of my own money, but I just can't find the courage. And a loyal part of me doesn't want to upset him by making him think I don't trust him.

'You can go now.' He waves me away. I hate him sometimes. 'Actually, on second thoughts, you can clean that up first, there's a good girl.'

He points to the ink and the blood, checks his reflection in the glass then leaves the office humming. I wait until I'm certain he's gone then give him the finger. Or at least I half give him it, before wondering if he can still see me somehow. He has that effect on everyone.

It was a bad night and now it's going to be a bad day. No sleep, fresh blood trickling down the nape of my neck, cleaning up my blood from the wall and Sid's spatters of ink from everywhere else. Threatened with the asylum. Giving up my bed to some random woman. Cast in what sounds like a séance act again.

From now on I'm calling Sid, Pernicious Sid.

3

The docks sweat no matter what time of day and morning is the busiest. People who've been working all night make their way home with bleary eyes and filthy faces. Coal workers trudge, black as night and phlegmy. Their rare smiles show teeth outlined by a permanent black grit, their nostrils black holes to their charred insides. The black gold they shovel sails money in from across the sea and powers the steamships out. I give a couple of them a 'hullo'. I'm down here a lot searching for clues, so I know a fair few.

The sun has cooked the smells already and I'm surrounded by smoke and fish, salt and baking, mud, bodies and grime. This is where I was found so I keep an extra sharp eye out for my mother here. I won't let the hope burn out. I've spotted her about fifteen times already. Every red-haired woman. Every woman wearing a hat, or a shawl over their heads, which is pretty much everyone. Every beggar and shadow and glimpse.

Mabel Jones is nattering to a group of girls by the sea lock. I don't really have time to join them but I can't help wanting to tell the story of my injuries.

'Mabel. Girls.' I let them take in the full glory of my cuts and bruises.

'What happened to you?' Ruth the Fish almost drops her basket.

'Oh, you know. This and that.' I'm going to play it as if I don't want to tell the story. Someone being genuinely interested in my life is such a change and I can't help basking in the warmth of the attention.

'Probably looking for her mother again and slipped on the bank or something.' Mabel is spiteful when she wants to be. Which is always.

'I am doing some investigative work, certainly. Not that you would want to know about it, and I am in a bit of a hurry, I'm afraid.' I've put Mabel's nose out of joint but she won't let me have the opportunity to fabricate a story on her watch.

'Well, we were just talking about the tunnel, weren't we, girls?' They murmur. I think most of them would rather listen to me but they are a pack and they stick together. 'It'll be open soon and there'll be a whole new set of boys over there.'

She giggles and points to Penarth, just the other side of the docks. They've been working on the tunnel under the River Ely for ages and it's set to open any day now. Mabel will be the first through it if she has her way. She gives me one of her most smug expressions. 'I thought you were in a rush to get somewhere? I presume it's incredibly important.'

One day I'm going to smash her squashed-up face in and be carried through the streets by the other girls in celebration that someone finally had the guts.

'You're right. Enjoy your day, girls.' I look at every one of them except her. It feels good to leave her out and then immediately bad. I shouldn't bully her just because she's a nincompoop. Her no-good father's done a runner and her mother's partial to a spot of gin and easy with her slaps.

I know where I'm headed. Some days it feels useless but I won't give up until the day I die. It can be dangerous down here. People could try to mug me for the very little that I have. I'd have to put up a fist fight. I'd give it a good go, but I'm no match for a gang, and people stick together here. Safety in numbers and all that. That's the way it should be. Like families protecting each other. One of the boys saw someone shot down here and looked straight through the hole in his body to England across the channel, but no one will dob the attacker in. That's the way it is here. Thick as thieves. Which most of them are.

I have that sick feeling that comes from having had no sleep and I have to stop and press my hands to my eyes to stay upright. I take a second to rest. The masts of the ships score the clear blue sky and gulls use them as perching places.

I love to swim but the water here is filled with rubbish and bits of discarded wood. It wouldn't come as a complete shock to find a body floating in it too. There are always stories about stuff like that. Bloated bodies. Their skin silver-blue. Their eyes eaten out by fish. Of course, it's always seen by a friend of a friend, and never by the person telling the story. There are better places to swim where I won't catch cholera, or bump into an eyeless corpse. They might be a bit of a walk away but I'd rather make the effort. Not now though.

The gash on my forehead is tingling, and my split lip must be reacting to the salt of the sea because it stings to Barry and back. I remove my gloves to try to cool down. They are encrusted with dirt and blood but I can't throw them away, so I pocket them in my skirt. I'll wash them out later and hope for the best.

'You alright there, love?' It's the woman I see hanging about drinking by the pubs. She can't get in anymore because she's been barred but they serve her through a hatch in most places.

'I'm fine, thanks.' I keep my wits about me. Her eyes keep flicking over me, more than likely looking for anything worth stealing.

'Lovely day.' The sky is the colour of a robin's egg but she is only trying to distract me.

'Lovely.' I shade my eyes and pretend to contemplate the sky. She adjusts her head so it's pointing upwards but her eyes are still straining over me. We stand there for a while pretending to admire the weather. To be fair it is usually pelting down on a bad day and drizzling on a good, so we should appreciate this rare occurrence. But we don't. We just use it to try to gain things for ourselves. Or at least she does. We stand there so long, I wonder if anyone will ever make the first move. A cormorant shakes coal dust from its wings then flies off low down to the water. Time reels itself out and yawns.

She says, 'Well, I'll be off then.' Hah, you wicked old witch, I win.

She swerves as she walks away and I worry that perhaps I judge people too quickly, and maybe she just wanted to pass the time of day with another human being. Then I see her reaching into the pocket of a man who is actually observing the sky and taking out his wallet. I don't tell him. Everyone needs to eat, and I'm impressed that even when she's so drunk she can still be nimble fingered.

I press on. If I can get to the river quickly then I might have the time to sleep a bit before I go back to the theatre. Steam from the trains just makes the day hotter. There is a shifting haze over the water, a thick mixture of coal and wood-smoke, and there are so many people jostling each other and vying for space. Sometimes I wonder how we all survive, there are so many of us fighting over so little.

I need to eat something but I haven't got a farthing on me. I'll just have to keep my head down and try to zone the world out, as I reach the river's edge. It's even brighter here. The sun sparkles to points of pain on the water.

'Hey! Be careful.' I tell one of the kids off as they accidentally run into me. I check my pockets but my gloves are still there.

A couple of tiny tots are playing with a wooden box which they are attempting to use as a boat in the sludge. A girl I've met down here before smokes a bashed-up cigar which the others are trying to take from her. She isn't giving in easily, and clips at them while they yip with laughter.

I look for my mother.

There are a few men flat out on the grass further up trying to get some kip, after a hard night's slog, no doubt. I pick my way around them, even checking that one of them isn't her in docker's clothes, dressed up like a man to get work for a fussy employer. She's not there.

A flock of women dart about, cuffing wearily at the nippers if they come too close and holding babies to their breasts. I check them. The thought that she might now have a new baby to take care of brings a lump to my throat.

I search the ground, the banks, the trees, the

water. Everywhere. Looking for anything. I don't even know what. I'm just hoping that something will strike a chord and lead me to her. A piece of material from her dress caught up somewhere. A coil of her hair in the branch of a tree.

A few of the mudlarks wave when they see me. We have an agreement. If they think they have found something that might be of any help to me, they will show me before selling it on, or pawning it. I will show them anything I find that might be worth some money as a form of payment. In the past few months I have found some buttons, a few bits of metal, some busted-up piano keys, lots of bottles – mostly broken, none containing messages from my mother – and some useful bits of wood. They are grateful enough for anything I find but haven't been able to help me yet. It is good to know that they are trying.

'Not found nothing yet?' It's Dylan. One of the boys I see down here lots.

'No. Have you?' I hope he can't see the jitter in my legs.

'Nothing yet.' He hops about from foot to foot like a jackdaw. 'But we'll keep a lookout for you, don't you worry. You look worse than usual.'

I laugh and my head swims. 'Well, thank you very much I'm sure.'

'Here.' He pulls half a bread roll from his ragged trousers.

I unfurl a fist and catch it as he tosses it to me. I bite into it ravenously. It's dry and takes considerable chewing. It sticks in my throat but I act like it's the best thing I ever ate. Food is hard to come by for this boy and I am grateful beyond words. There's a whistle in the distance, followed by another closer, and then another closer still.

'Time to go.' He gives me a mock salute. Like I said, people down here work together. They signal with whistles when the coppers are on their way. I guess most of them have done something on the dodgy side of the law. I see the policemen's pointed helmets in the distance. Sid has warned me off confiding in the police about my mother. He says they will take me into custody and have me adopted to somewhere so far away that if she ever came back she would never, ever find me.

I think about my options for a second then scarper like the rest of them.

4

Violet Night is so ugly she looks as if she has a false nose. Her eyebrows are drawn in high above where a person's eyebrows naturally should be and her mouth is a tight purple slash across her face. So far, I've been shown to her like a cut of pork hanging in a butcher's and she has eyed me up and down, before being led away on her grand tour by Sid, who turned back to glare at me as if I'd done something wrong. Which I probably have.

'I vant you to do somesing for me, little geeeeeeerrrrrrrrrrllllll!' Constance, the magician's assistant, has also arrived and it seems her secret talent is impersonations. She has Violet Night down to a T. 'Ah yes. I am Mizz Violet Night. I am from some never heard of country somewhere out zare in ze unlucky world. I walks about quickly to avoid ze stinks of ze normal peoples.'

Constance paces the room as if she has a broom handle stuck up her bum. Her lip curls as she pretends to smell me. 'I have eyes in ze back of my head!'

She purposely walks backwards into the wall and then rubs at her scalp. I am weak with laughing so much. I can hardly breathe.

'Stop … please … I can't take any more.' It's the truth. I have so little cause for laughter these days I'd forgotten how much effort was involved.

'I talk to ze dead.' There's a head of a mannequin in the corner and she boots it across the room. 'You! You dead peoples. Get up. Stop being so lazy.'

My sides are aching. I think Constance is delighted to have such an avid audience. She's already told me she thinks she is wasted as a magician's assistant. She puts a penny in her eye socket and tries to hold it there, pretending it's a monocle. It keeps slipping out and watching her scrabble about on the floor for it just makes me laugh harder.

'Where are you, you dead peoples? I can't find you. Stop hiding from me, you naughty dead persons!' She stretches her hands out in front of her. 'When I get hold of you dead peoples I will bore you with my completely made-up powers.'

She makes a grab for me and though I try to run away, there isn't far to go in my room. I should call it *our* room now.

'Are you a dead persons? You feel a bit warm to me.'

I like Constance already. She arrived this morning and as soon as I met her we started laughing.

She doesn't seem to be fazed by anything. She told Sid we needed some time to get to know each other. Then, when we got to my room, she said I looked dead on my feet so I was to go to sleep for a couple of hours while she got settled in. She's refused to take my bed and said she'll manage with the old sackcloth thing Sid had intended me to use. I didn't put up much of an argument. It's only a mattress on top of some broken pallets but my bed is one of the only things I count as mine. When I woke up from my nap I was happy to see she was still here.

Constance is savvy in a way I hope to be one day.

'What's London like?' I've always wanted to go there and Constance has travelled all over.

'It's big, Nan.' She sits on a crate then beckons me over to curl her hair into loops. 'And it's dirty. There's more people there than you can possibly imagine. And it smells really, really, really bad.'

'It sounds wonderful.'

She laughs at me. I laugh too. I suppose it must seem weird to want to go to somewhere that smells so awful.

'You feeling a bit better?' She observes me in the blotchy mirror.

'Much.' My head has stop bleeding. My lip hasn't swollen as badly as it could have. My arms are covered by my dress and if I can't see the bruises I can't really feel them hurting as much.

I say, 'My mother is missing.'

'Aw, petal.' She is only half listening and I can tell that she doesn't really register what I say, so great is her concentration on showing me where to pin her hair. To take my mind off my troubles, I begin to imagine myself on the London stage, taking my final encore as posies rain down on me. The smell of success fills the auditorium, alongside lavender perfumes and earthy pungent cigars.

I come back from the daydream to find that she is pleased with my work.

'Righty-oh, Nan. We'd better get up there to that sod.'

We make our way to the stage. I'm dressed as a small child again. Constance is lucky that she's allowed to dress as a woman. She's not that much older than me but she clearly has a world of experience that she wears like armour.

'Let's have a quick smoke.' She stops on the stairs and pulls a clay pipe from a pocket in the side of her skirt. 'Never be without it.'

Her wink crinkles the side of her eyes, betraying years of mischief.

'I don't. But thanks.' If I'm honest it makes me feel like I'm going to catch fire. I tried it once and I swear it took the skin off the inside of my oesophagus. 'I might go on up.'

I've seen Sid's reaction to people being late.

'Listen.' She takes a deep puff and releases it in rings. The tobacco burns bright then smoulders. 'You have to learn how to control men like Pernicious Sid.' She titters at the name as she says it. 'You have to learn how to play them like a violin.'

'It's not the same for me.' Sid has known me too long. 'He practically brought me up.'

'Dragged you up more like.'

I take a bit of offence at this. I've done pretty well all things considered. But I like her and we've only just met. I don't want to fall out with her already. I have to share a room with her and I'm all for trying to make my life a little bit easier. I giggle but it's false.

I check about us and try to waft her smoke so it disappears. 'He'll kill you for smoking down here. He's really strange about it.'

'He's really strange about everything. But point taken. I'm not really ready to be killed just yet.' She laughs, then coughs so hard she has to thump herself in the chest.

'Hey!' I almost jump out of my skin as Bee appears from nowhere. 'Bee. You didn't half give me a shock. Can't you get heavier boots or something?'

It is a gag between us that she is as quiet as a mouse and able to sneak about undetected if she chooses.

'You should give up smoking. It's not good for you.' Even though she looks the picture of innocence, I can tell by Bee's voice that she hasn't taken to Con. I give her my best 'behave' look. She retorts with an even sweeter smile.

'Don't be silly, duck. The pharmacist told me it'd clear my chest.'

'Well, you shouldn't smoke down here because that's definitely not good for you if Sid finds out.'

'It's like the smoking police here, innit?' Constance hacks again then wheezes.

'This is Beerlulla.' I smile sweetly back at Bee and get a thwack across my arm for it. 'She likes to be called Bee because everyone thinks her real name makes her sound soft. And she certainly isn't.'

I narrowly dodge another thwack.

'That's alright. I like to be called Con. I'm not sweet neither.' Constance stubs her ash out with her thumb. 'Anyway, thanks for the warning, doll. I'll be careful not to be caught. Right, we better get up there or the Great Pathetico will be having kittens.'

She is talking about the magician she works with. She's already complained that his tricks are old hat, which is a shame as I like magic when it's good. I hoick up my little child bloomers. Constance taps the remains of her pipe out of the window and we hear a yell from someone who must have been standing below.

'Come on!' Shrieking with laughter and tossing her hair over her shoulder, Constance grabs hold of my hand.

'Bye, Bee. See you later!' I don't want Bee to think that Constance could ever replace her as my best friend so I make a face behind Constance's back. It makes Bee laugh but I feel immediately guilty. I prefer to be nice to people. When I can.

We race up the stairs, looking behind us dramatically as if someone with a singed head is going to be right at our heels, just larking about for the hell of it. When we get to the side of the stage we are sweaty and breathless, and the 'Great Pathetico' is already waiting on stage with a saw in his hand, seemingly dumbstruck by the lack of a woman to saw in half.

'I'm fashionably late as usual.' Constance struts on to the boards with all the glamour of a leading lady arriving for her adoring fans. After a largely inaudible but clearly heated exchange, she climbs into the gaudily painted box and gives a lame shriek of agony. She then yawns melodramatically and grins across at me. I have to admit, even though I hardly know her at all yet, I love her don't care attitude, and she clearly values herself above anyone else.

'Alright, Nan?' It's Henry, one of the stagehands. He looks me up and down and I know he is about to tease the life out of me. It's so unfair for girls. Boys get to do all the great jobs and we get to do nothing good at all.

'The important role of the child again, is it?' His impishness flickers in his eyes as he glances at me, then watches the onstage antics.

'Child skipping this time. It's a very important part I'll have you know.'

He laughs, though I get the sense he is only half listening. 'She's a firecracker, isn't she?'

He's talking about Constance, who has now made it out of the cabinet alive and is balanced on one leg with the other leg held up in the air for some reason.

'Yeah. Con's just fine. We're really good friends already.'

'Are you? That's good.'

I can feel a rash coming up on my neck from this stupid outfit. I need to swim. I think of plunging myself headfirst into the water, the coldness cleansing me, making me cool and pure and clever and new.

'I was wondering…'

'What?' My voice is chilled with a sharp knife edge. I hate being stopped when I'm swimming. Even if I am only imagining it.

'There's this Magic Lantern show on Saturday. Do you think she'd want to go with me?'

'I shouldn't think so. You're an idiot.'

He doesn't say anything. He just looks me up and down, then saunters off and chats with some of the stagehands.

Dust motes sprinkle the space between us like tiny sea sparkles. The world is heavenly, and beautiful, and feathered. Filled with possibility. I love the Magic Lantern show above almost everything else. I imagine the glow of the lantern slides as they light up in the darkness. The tragically beautiful women and the endlessly villainous men. I'll take Bee with me. It will be glorious.

A screeching noise pierces my bubble. Sid's voice.

'Where on earth is she?'

Damn. I hadn't noticed the magician's act finish and I've missed my cue where I'm supposed to skip across the stage. The dancing girls have stopped hoofing away and are all staring at me and whispering behind their hands. The jaunty piano music has halted. There's nothing theatre people like more than a good show, whether it is scripted or no.

I take a few teetering steps on to the stage, trying not to twist my ankle in the grooves in the floor they slide the scenery on. I feel smaller than the child I'm dressed up to be.

'Nansi, my love. Where have you been?' His face is danger red. His lips blue-white and snarling. It doesn't take much to make him apoplectic, especially from me.

'I…' My words give up on me. My throat's as dry as tailor's chalk and getting drier by the second.

'I'm sorry, Sid.' A voice rings out clear as a bell from behind me. 'It's just I needed help to stitch these back up where the stupid sod has sawed through them again.'

Constance holds up a pair of her bloomers which are now sliced through at the front. The dancers fall about in hilarity, breaking the atmosphere, and even Sid conjures a toothy guffaw.

'I didn't realise it was her cue coming up. My fault entirely. Sorry, doll.' She tosses her hair flirtatiously. 'I can make it up to you if you like, Sid?'

Someone in the wings gives a 'whit-whoo' and there is a fresh round of hysterics. Sid's grin spreads from one oily ear to the other and only people who know him as well as I do would realise it was an act.

'It's fine, Constance my sweet,' he simpers at her. 'But we must let the lesser girls do their bit.'

I hate to be made fun of like this. Like I'm nothing. Less than nothing.

'Just make sure you don't do it again.' There's an edge to his voice that everyone recognises. Sid never has to tell people twice.

Constance licks her scarlet lips slowly then smiles. 'I wouldn't dream of it, Sid.'

As she turns away from him, she rolls her eyes at me. She doesn't realise that Sid can see her expression in the piano player's mirror, but I do. I catch the spite in his quickly covered reaction. She'll pay for this.

'Nansi. Office.'

It seems my time as a small girl skipping is over for the day and I know I should be happy but I'm filled with dread.

5

Violet Night's eyebrows go in every direction but across. She wears what looks like a black wedding dress. Perhaps she became a medium because she was widowed. Perhaps someone really loved her once. I look at her eyebrows again and decide not.

She and Sid are deep in whispered conversation. I'm stood in the corner as if I'm awaiting execution. I only came up to deliver some notes from Stage Door and Sid told me to stay put because he'd be needing me shortly anyway. I should've sent someone else with them but no one wanted to do it. I'm a nincompoop like that.

There's a reluctant knock at the door. I know that way of knocking. Where you hope it is quiet enough that you won't be heard at all.

'Entrez,' Sid answers immediately, which almost makes me faint in surprise.

Bee comes in warily, then, seeing me, looks relieved and scoots to my side. I am alarmed.

'What's she doing here?' I should know better than to question. I should have learned to bite my tongue. It breaks up the huddle Sid and Violet Night have been in. Sid seems happy, which is even more worrying.

'I've been telling Ms Night what a charming seamstress young Bee is.'

Bee pushes herself closer to my side. I take Bee's hand. She has tiny blood spots on her thumbs and fingers where she has pricked herself with a needle. She says you get used to the pain after a while.

'Ms Night would like to talk to you about a costume, Bee, so listen well, there's a darling.'

I glower at Sid for his patronising tone but keep my mouth shut. Violet takes the monocle which is hanging from a chain around her neck and puts it to her eye to examine Bee, who quite naturally cowers even more, though she tries not to show it.

'What's wrong with the costumes we already have?' I am taking my life in my hands here, but Bee is like my sister and I'm appealing to his better nature (I'm certain there must be one deep down).

'I'm not talking to you, so do me a favour and shut it.'

Sid puts his hand out to Bee. She knows better than to ignore it. It's a sickening sight, his gnarled old digits hooked into her like that. 'Now, Bee, this nice lady here wants a very special dress.'

Bee eyes him. She has a sullen look about her.

'And I've told her you have the sweetest, most beautiful needlework skills in the whole of Wales.'

If anything, this makes Bee even more sullen.

'So no pressure or anything.' I try to make a joke of it. I just can't stop myself.

Sid looks as if he might pick up the nearest heavy object and hurl it at me, but he is trying to impress Violet Night.

'So, Bee, give her an idea of how absolutely stupendous you are.' He drops her hand and leaves her standing in the centre of the office while he leans back against his desk and waits. It's stifling in here. Bee opens and shuts her mouth like a goldfish but no sound comes out.

'Come on now Bee. Nothing to be afraid of. Tell her about the kind of costumes you've made. You know, styles, that sort of thing.' The way Sid says this implies that there is everything to be afraid of. Bee's staring at Violet Night as if she is in a hypnotic trance. Sid's foot is starting to twitch.

'It's alright, Bee.' I scoop her under my arm. 'I'll tell Ms Night how good you are. Though I don't know why she hasn't brought her own collection of costumes like everyone else.'

Most touring artistes have a chest of things they drag along with them. Sid must really rate this woman if he's willing to foot the bill for her.

'This is wasting my time.' Violet drops the monocle and glares at Sid. 'I thought you said this Bee girl, or whatever her name is, was from overseas so she would be able to create something unique.'

I stifle a laugh. Bee's mother was Somalian but she was born in Cardiff docks. Sid stunts me with a look.

'She will make you something most spectacular indeed.' Sid scrapes the chair from beneath his desk. 'Please sit, my dear Ms Violet.'

She sits like a mardy five year old.

'Take a pen, dear lady, and draw for us what you had envisioned, that we may understand your genius better.'

I glance in Bee's direction. She is as flabbergasted

as I am. The only reason I can imagine that Sid would be so slimy with this woman, and I'm trying really hard not to think it, is that he fancies her. Bee puts both her hands over her heart as if she is swooning. I make a vomiting action in response. We try not to crack up with laughter.

'It will have a bodice like this.' Violet Night's eyebrows make the shape of a capital V as she concentrates. 'And it will go out here.'

She draws a big shock of material down from the waist. As she sketches, I can't help but notice that on every finger she has gold rings encrusted with diamonds and opals, pearls, rubies, sapphires and jet. That would explain it then. The woman has money. I look over at Bee and her expression shows that she has also clocked the jewels. I pretend to scratch my neck, meaning to look at the collection of chains and beads and gems of Violet's necklaces too.

'With some feathers here. And a sash here.'

She's not the best artist I've ever seen but it isn't entirely bad. I could imagine myself looking quite remarkable in it.

'And it will have thousands of sequins.'

Sid flinches a little. He is probably totting up

the cost of this garment as she adds more and more to it. I caught sight of his accounting books the other day and the theatre is in more debt than he'd care to admit. I study him slyly. He seems to be clinging to this old sow as if she is his only hope.

'And hundreds of beads here.'

I give Bee a sympathetic look.

'Of course, my dearest lady.' He smarms so much I want to slap him.

'And it will be green.'

'No.' The word is out before I can stop it.

'Nansi. Where are your manners? I apologise for the outburst, Ms Night. But as it distresses the poor lamb so, does it really have to be green?' Sid presumes I am afraid because green brings bad luck and he's thinking of ticket sales. But I have more real fears.

'Yes. Green. It's a necessity. I want it to match my eyes.'

She is an evil horse and I hate her. Green clothes are made with arsenic. People die from making them. Slow, painful, agonising deaths. Everyone knows it. She knows it.

I look at Bee. The colour has drained from her

54

face. I plead with Sid with my eyes. Surely, he can convince this woman to wear a different colour? Surely, he will tell her to go somewhere else if she is this fussy.

'Then you shall have it.'

I wince at his words and remember that he is no friend of ours. I have got to find my mother so that we can get away.

'Now, I have business to which I must attend.' Sid reaches for his cane from the hatstand, then turns to give Violet his best dazzling look (I know he practises these looks in front of the mirror). 'Of course, I won't be needing you to come along, dear lady. Please take time to relax and enjoy the beauty of our theatre and the surrounding area.'

He takes Violet's hand and kisses it, then turns to Bee. 'You can get back to your sewing…'

Bee turns to leave.

'…a bit later than usual. First you are both coming out with me.'

Bee and I are perplexed. Sid never takes us anywhere. She gives me a quizzical look and I pull an expression that lets her know that it will be fine whatever happens. I would fight tooth and nail to protect her. I will have to make the dress myself, even if it will be a complete shambles and I do die from the arsenic. On second thoughts, I don't fancy dying that much. I must come up with a plan.

6

Sid moves at a pace out through the foyer and into the street. It's busy, as usual, as we race to keep up with him. I see lots of the faces I always see. The man who sells the *South Wales Echo* has been on his stand every day since I can remember. He gives me a cheery wave, then points at the headline on the front of the stand and shakes his head in disbelief, as he does every time I see him. The woman begging on the street corner gives me a nod. I try to share my food with her as often as I can. Her name is Amelia Longthorne and she was happy once. She never tells me what brought her here and I don't like to pry.

'Where are we going?' I almost tumble off the kerb and into the path of an oncoming omnibus as I try to keep level with him. Bee yanks me back at the last moment. Sid doesn't even break his stride.

'Don't be tiresome, Nansi. You'll see when we get there.'

Before I knew better I would have imagined perhaps he was going to take us for a row on Roath Park Lake. Or for an ice cream and out to sea on a pleasure steamer from Penarth pier. Now I don't even bother to let these happy thoughts in. One day I will take myself and Bee off for days out in those places and find happiness by my own means. For now, I have to keep earning money to put towards my detective. I wonder if I have enough to employ a dressmaker? I wonder if I can talk Violet Night into wearing something different? Perhaps one of the beauties Con has in her case? I'm hoping we might, by some strange miracle, spot the dress that Violet Night was describing so that I can steal it, not that I've ever stolen from a shop before.

We trot along like obedient ponies, me checking every passing woman just in case, Bee enthralled by the window displays. Waxen women sitting in deckchairs with parasols and bathing-suited children playing at their feet. China dolls and teddy bears in sailor suits. Shiny wheeled perambulators and copper-handled tin baths. Pharmacies and toyshops and a milliners with hats of all descriptions. And then, the bookshop. Oh! The bookshop. So many beautiful books in golds, and blues and greens. Silvers and purple. So many stories rattling about behind the glass. One day I will read all of those books and go on those adventures.

'Come on, Nansi. Stop ogling things that are none of your business.' Sid grabs me by the arm then tips his top hat to a woman who looks at us with concern. I smile to reassure her. We've been taught to do this, Bee and me. It's much better than a hiding.

We head towards the castle and beyond, across the river Taff and towards the cathedral. It's just like Sid to make us walk this far. Any normal person would have flagged down a hansom cab but he is too stingy. It's good for Bee to be out though. Getting some fresh air and seeing the sun and a bit of life, even if she is having to walk mile after mile to earn it.

'Right then. Both of you. Do me a favour and try to look inconspicuous.' We stop at the end of a well-to-do street. 'Nansi. This is your house. Understood?'

I nod. There is nothing else required.

I look at Bee. By trying to look inconspicuous, she is making herself more noticeable. Not many people walk about with their chins down to their chests. She notices me watching her and makes the most hilariously rude face at me.

Sid bids 'Good day' to the very people he is planning to steal from. 'I'm helping you, Nansi, because it's very important you have the right one. Aren't you going to thank me?'

'Thanks.' I add the next bit under my breath. 'For letting me rob people for you.'

'There's no need for sarcasm.' The man is as sharp as a tack and has the ears of a bat.

An elegant lady passes wearing a tussie-mussie of brightly coloured flowers on her waistband. Her dress is a Paris Emerald Green. Sid makes sure that Bee notices its colour and fear and nausea flood through me from my crown to my toes.

'You look pale, my sweet.' We have come to the end of the tree-lined avenue. 'You wait here and Bee and I will come back for you.'

He indicates that I am to sit on a bench that has been set out for the public with a view of the spires and the beautiful river beyond. It's so tempting to do what he asks and sit here a while, but I don't trust him to look after Bee one bit.

'I'm alright, thanks Sid. I'll come along with you.'

'It wasn't a request. Wait there.' I sit. Bee goes off with him, looking over her shoulder as he struts off in front of her. Sycamore seeds twirl around me and leaves rock gently down to the ground as I try not to think about sleep.

I wait till they turn out of the road and then leap up and race the length of the avenue. Peeping around the corner, I can see that Sid is also peering back. I manage to hide before he spies me. He doesn't trust me any more than I trust him.

I wait a moment, my heart thudding against my chest, my breath short and sharp. When I figure enough time has gone past, I look around again and see that they are far away in the distance. I run as fast as I can, with my hat held to the back of my head, ducking behind every available tree, pillar box and lamp post I can use as camouflage.

I don't think I've been up here before, it's quite a long way from town and I don't get much free time.

I'm sure it would be beautiful if my hair wasn't matted to me with sweat and panic. Eventually Sid turns off the main thoroughfare and through a gate. I dash again to keep up, trying not to draw attention to myself as I know I'll be back later for more criminal reasons. Why would he bring Bee here? And why doesn't he want me to see it? It makes no sense. I run through all the options in my head and come up with nothing. I study the place for clues.

The path seems so inviting. It reminds me of something from a dream or a story. I can see myself dancing down it into another world of love and laughter. This doesn't give me any help, however. Through the trees I can just make out a tower and I imagine myself a Rapunzel at the top, looking out and wanting to be free. Searching the skyline of Cardiff for the promise of a happy ending. This doesn't help me work out what Sid is up to either.

I sprint back to the bench where Sid and Bee left me. I'm dripping with sweat when I get there. In the distance I can see the inviting grey glint of the river. I wish I could go there now and throw myself into its waters. Instead I lay down on the bench, cover my face with my hat and act as if I'm asleep. I'm shaken awake soon enough.

'What? What is it? Huh?' I pretend to be befuddled. I make an excellent act of it, if I say so myself. 'Oh, Sid. Bee. You gave me a fright there, I was just having a snooze.'

'Clearly. Now let's go.'

I hate having to scamper after him but there seems little choice. Bee hasn't caught my eye yet but she looks troubled.

'Did you have a nice time without me?' I am hideously exhausted from running but trying to look nonchalant.

'Splendid, thank you.'

'That's good.' I pretend to be fascinated by a passing chimney sweep who is covered from head to toe in soot, the chirruping chaffinches flitting from garden to garden, my own feet. 'Where did you go, Bee?'

Sid doesn't give her a chance to respond. 'Why don't you mind your own business for a change, eh? Be a new experience for you.'

I smart at this. Even though he is often vindictive I still can't bear it when he directs his cruelty at me. We walk on in silence. Birds tweet in the trees as if there is nothing wrong.

'Sid has asked me to do a job, that's all.' Bee says

it offhandedly. As if she breaks into houses and steals for him every night. I know it's a front.

'I'll do it.'

'You have quite enough on.'

'I don't mind, Sid. Really I don't. I'm quick and practised and I'll get it done so fast...'

'You'll do as you're told.' He lifts his cane as if he is thinking of thrashing me with it then realises we are in a public area. 'Anyway, you don't know where the house is, my dear. So I'm afraid, in spite of your good intentions, you can't.'

Oh, but I do, Sid. I do. I hug this piece of knowledge close to my chest. It's good to have one over on Sid, however small it may be. He struts along all the way back, attempting to give off the air of a real gentleman and turning his nose up at urchins who beg him for money.

As we go, Sid quietly explains Violet Night's act to me. I'll visit the houses of rich families who are mourning their dead, like the house he showed me. I'll use the trick of dressing as a maid to get in and then snoop about to steal a trinket or two for Violet to use in her medium act. The recently bereaved don't need much cajoling to believe that a sign has been sent by their loved one. And who would believe that anyone would be so low as to steal from these mourning families? Sid is hoping it will help to draw the crowds in and make him money. If it doesn't make enough, he'll have someone rob their houses while they are out for the evening. So, dead people are a part of the act but not in the way they usually are. I don't have to dress up as a ghost, for which I am grateful. But I don't like Bee having any part in it and the whole thing is sick and vile anyway. Playing on people's emotions like that and using the loss of their children to make money. On the other hand, Sid says that if I do well I won't have to do so much other thieving.

By the time we get to the theatre we are all exhausted.

'Right then, girls. I'm off to have an afternoon nap. You get on with your work.'

I can't say how tired I am, as Sid would know I hadn't been sleeping while he was casing the house with Bee.

'Bee. Ms Night's dress needs to be breathtaking, you hear me? She needs to look absolutely stunning.'

'Bee doesn't have that long.'

Bee snorts with laughter. Sid ignores me and ushers her off.

'Nansi. Go and get on with whatever it is you do around here before I question why I pay to keep a roof over your head.' He catches his reflection in one of the framed posters in the foyer and seems distinctly pleased by it. 'You can have a night off tonight. You've done well.'

I almost faint with shock.

'But don't expect another one. We don't want you getting lazy, now do we?'

He dismisses me without a backward glance. I stomp off to my room, which is childish, I know, but I work so hard and he never seems to appreciate anything. A night off is a chink of happiness, though. Perhaps he just finds it hard to show his real feelings?

Checking that no one has followed me, I take out Bee's copy of *Grimm's Fairy Tales* and settle down in my corner to read. I call it Bee's copy but really it is on an unauthorised loan from that house I pilfered from. I will take it back as soon as I can but for now I need to read to cheer myself up. The bit in *Cinderella* where the stepmother forces one sister to chop off her heels and the other to chop off her toes is good. I'm glad that the pigeons called out to the prince to notice the blood on their shoes before he married them. It's good to know that nature is on Cinderella's side. I gently wrap the book in the blanket and put it into the trunk. It feels good to take care of something properly.

My head is filled with confusion and doubt. All I know is that I can't let Bee down. There's no way I'd let her go and get caught red-handed taking things from that house. I can't figure why Sid wants her to do it instead of me. Perhaps he is just trying to recruit her to that side of things. Well, tough luck, Sid. I'll do it myself. Perhaps I can steal something which I can pawn to pay for a dressmaker too. It's a brilliant idea. And I'll make sure I get them their property back one day, somehow. If I can give everything back, I won't feel like I need to swim far from the shore. Swim and swim into the channel and let the current take me. Let the water wash out all the bad.

7

Sid's kept to his word about the extra thieving and even if I know it won't last, I was glad of a night off. Even if Constance did come in and catch me flat out asleep with the book on my face. I hide my reading if I can. It's embarrassing and people tease me. Constance said I was wasting my time with it. You don't need to read to be on the stage. She's right but I still love the stories. I carry them in my mind like old friends and I feel as if I've known the characters all my life.

The theatre was dark last night. There was no show and I had the opportunity to do something I really enjoyed. I didn't have the energy to make it to the lake so I went as far as the paddling pool at Victoria Park, which might make you laugh but sometimes just enough water to float in can do the trick. I suddenly remembered learning to float there in the first place. I sucked the air into my lungs and let my tummy ease up to the surface till my toes popped through it and my hands gently paddled while I explored my newfound freedom. My mother was wearing teal-green satin the day I learnt. Her hair bounced against it in spirals. The memory of her face is a rippled reflection. I clutch at the few memories I do have, like cobwebs spun from the finest glass. They are so few and so precious.

I could feel the tears dripping sideways down my face and joining with the pool. I imagined they were all my bad feelings leaking away and that kind of made me feel better. Well, enough to sleep anyway, so I've had some actual rest to prepare me for this scam. I'm still not comfortable with it. Who would be? But at least I'm fairly safe scouting about as a maid busy with chores. These big houses have so many maids these days no one can keep track of who is who.

I've made it into the main hall of the house Sid showed me, by slipping in through the scullery then walking with purpose, and am now rubbing at the silver from one of their display cabinets with a chamois leather. Whenever anyone comes anywhere close, I try to look fully engrossed in my work. Even though it's only part of the act I'm proud of the way the sun gleams on the metal, as a shaft of light from the window bounces off it and creates a scatter of tiny rainbow fairies on the wall. I make them dance across the rose-patterned wallpaper, glint through the sombre gilt framed paintings, past the jade and gold grandfather clock with the etching of the happy full moon, till they reach the door of the parlour where the corpse is laid.

A man in there is taking a photograph of the family with the dead girl. I saw the elder sister being taken in there against her will. He dipped his head beneath the cloth on the camera, his legs splayed at a strange angle not to tip over the tripod, and then the door slammed unceremoniously in my face. They will probably have the image framed or set in jewellery of some kind. The air is thick with the smell of leather and I'm glad of the patch of forget-me-not blue sky beyond the round window high above me.

'What do you think you are doing?' A woman pinches my arm hard and I spin like a cat ready to scratch. 'You're supposed to be cleaning. Not daydreaming.'

'I wasn't. I mean … I am cleaning. I was just checking this would sparkle in the sun.'

'Well, more elbow grease and less frolics.' She walks imperiously towards a far door and disappears below stairs without another glance. She has no idea who I am. I have no idea who she is. For all I know she might be another scammer working for another Sid.

I pick up a candelabra, even though I've already done it once. I'm waiting for a chance to sneak upstairs to find a personal trinket, but people keep moving in and out of the mourning room. As this is my first job for Violet's act, I don't want to bungle it. I hear hushed voices and keep my head low as a mark of respect as they pass. Mostly so they don't speak to me or question who I am. They probably wouldn't in a residence this big, but you can never be too careful.

I can hear people chattering outside in the street as if nothing is happening here. Noises from the kitchen scamper up the stairs. A less stern clock chimes somewhere. I am on the point of doing a runner when there is a loud screech from the mourning room. A butler hurries out and someone shouts at him to fetch a doctor immediately. I know it's my time. With all this kerfuffle no one will pay the slightest heed to my actions.

I'm up the stairs in seconds, looking for the girl's room. She wasn't an infant so it won't be a corridor off the master bedroom. It won't be too far up into the attics as the servants sleep there. It will be one of the rooms ahead of me, I'm certain. I put my ear to one closed door and, hearing nothing, open it cautiously. It's a bedroom, but not a child's. Possibly the governess's as there are books and lady's clothes. I try again. Another bedroom, but this time a boy's. A row of tin soldiers have been abandoned mid battle. I quash the urge to put them straight.

Third time lucky, I hope. I press my ear to a third door. Nothing. I slip through. This is the right room, without question. The bed is unmade as if someone has recently been lifted from it. There is a rocking horse gathering dust near the window and a tapestry above the bed reads 'Miranda'. The girl's name. I feel sick, but pretend to myself it is lack of sleep. Knowing her name makes her so real.

I need to take something that is personal but won't be too hurtful to the mother.

Here and there about the room there are cards with drawings of the sea. I could take one of these. They are beautiful but they seem so loved. So particularly chosen that I can't bring myself to lay a finger on them. Jewellery? Also too personal. I imagine her wearing those pearls around her neck at a party and quickly shake the image away. I'm not good at this. It just feels so wrong. And yet I have no choice. There must be something that won't be too keenly missed.

I scan the room again. In a jar on the window ledge is a collection of small blue and white pieces of sea glass. Perfect. I love these myself. She and I could have been friends in different circumstances.

A squirrel jumps from the tree just beyond the window and I see my reflection against the growing dark outside. I'm not who I was meant to be. I am this shadow of the girl I once was.

Stepping back from my image, I shut my heart to this family's plight. I have too many problems of my own to worry for the world.

'You, girl.'

I almost jump right out of my skeleton but recover myself rapidly and turn to answer an authoritative man with my best wide-eyed innocent expression. I think I overdo it a little, so tone it down. Again, I can't help but enjoy the adrenalin of acting and I hate myself for it. 'Me, sir?'

'You're not supposed to be in here.' He jabs me accusingly in the shoulder. I wish that I could clout him one back.

'Oh, I'm sorry, sir, I'm sorry.' I play the flustered maid part so well. Keeping my head down I scurry around him to the door.

'Stop right there.'

I'm rumbled. My skin scalds. I get ready to run.

He sighs. 'It's hard on all of us. Try to keep a brave face on it, there's a girl.'

I nod with my eyes downcast. He has mistaken my pitying myself for grief for the girl. I feel like I'm slathered in layers of filth. My insides feel hollow. I don't know who I am anymore. I don't know who I'm supposed to be.

I dash away from the house, struggling to get a breath of fresh air that will clear my lungs of the taste of death and wrong. I get as far as the wrought-iron gate of the house Bee has been told to rob in a kind of daze. This happens to me sometimes. If stuff gets too much I switch off. I can keep going, and going, and going, not thinking of anything other than how much sweat I am creating. How the liquid pouring out of me will wash the horrible feelings away when I swim later.

Bee said there's only one house down that drive so it'll be easy enough to find. They don't have a bereaved person there. This is normal thieving but for a change Sid has been very specific about what he wants taken and where it is.

Bee told me there is a pond in the back terrace of the garden. Next to the pond is a stone wall. She was told to look for the stone with the tiny gold star painted on it. There's a casket hidden there. It all sounds very peculiar.

There is no one about, which is a small miracle, so I work speedily. The pond is easy to find, a delightful thing covered in lily pads. It would be really lovely to dip my feet into, if only I had the time.

It reminds me of something. A picture I have seen in a fairy tale book perhaps? It's so comforting and warm and familiar. This whole place has such a nice atmosphere. I feel as if I could lay down here and go to sleep, gently, safely.

Of course I can't and it is just a fancy, so I get back to the task in hand.

It takes me a while to locate the star. It's not gold anymore. I suppose it has been ravaged by the weather, now it is the green which grows on copper. Between the moss and lichen coating the wall I am lucky to find it at all. The stone budges after a bit of coaxing and sure enough there is a casket behind it. I check around again. Apart from a gardener a long way off talking to some carrots he is growing, I seem to be alone. I'm hidden from the house here. It couldn't be more perfect. I wrestle the casket from its hiding place and hurriedly place the stone back.

Usually I would wait to get back to the theatre to check my haul. This time I don't. It's just so intriguing and I'm eager to find out what is so precious. I let myself out through a gate and then sit on my haunches with my back against the garden wall and the casket in my lap. It is a grand thing, made to look like a pirate's treasure chest, but a bit grubby and knockabout from its recent hiding place.

I prise it open. A wooden model of a boat. Obviously much loved and with watermarks as if it has been launched several times. A few drawings of a girl and a few drawings of a boy. Both of them have been made to look like caricatures, for fun I suppose, and both drawn by different hands. I imagine they were drawing each other. Sid can't want these. Beneath them there is a roll of banknotes tightly held together with a rubber band. That makes more sense. And a velvet drawstring pouch. I open it and sure enough it is filled with jewellery and charms. It must be worth a fair penny but I don't have the skills to tot it up.

On a whim I take out a locket and snap the clasp open. There is a lock of yellow hair in there, baby hair, I would think, by how soft and new it looks. I can't let Sid have that. It would be too much to hide the entire collection of jewellery but this must be precious to someone. I'll pawn it and get it back to its rightful owner somehow.

More blissful than anything else is what lays along the bottom of the casket. A copy of Andersen's fairy tales. There is no way on earth that Sid would be interested in this, his disregard for books is irritating, to say the least. He won't mind if I have it for myself. One day I'll put it back.

While I'm doing this, I've left Bee hidden in my room at the theatre looking at the pictures in the books. Even though she is only still learning to read, she loves the shape of the letters and the sketches. It took a bit of a squabble to convince her to stay behind, but I'm stubborn when I want to be and she was mollified by the fact that she can repay the favour another time. She won't be asked to but that's beside the point. Con will cover for her if Sid turns up, so I know she's fairly safe.

My sweat smells like sharp onions by the time I get back to town. I'll swim later if I get the chance. I'm not going to go straight to Sid. I'm too exhausted.

There are lots of backstage boys shuffling about. Carrying bits and pieces, banging together flats of scenery and touching up props where the paint has been scuffed. I try to slip by unnoticed, keeping my arms close to my body to avoid letting the smell eek out. It would be horrendous if a rumour started about the way I pong. When I get to my room I strip my clothes off, trying to ignore the chill, and nestle down beneath my threadbare blanket to look through the book I have taken.

I am so in the thrall of the story of *The Little*

Mermaid that when the door bursts open I realise I have been so engrossed I have let the blanket slide.

'Argh.' I try to cover myself even though I'm not completely nude. I'm embarrassed by almost every bit of me, none of it is right and all of it is awkward.

It's Constance, thank goodness. She clearly isn't expecting me to be here as she throws her pipe up in the air in shock. Sparks glitter the floor for a moment as it lands then burn out like tiny dying stars. She stands stock still in the doorway as if she has seen a vision. I look down at myself. My knees are pretty horrendous and scabbed. I cover them.

'Are you feeling alright? I know I'm not particularly attractive but that seems a bit of an overreaction?' I try to make light of it but she still stares at me as if I am in a Freak Show. Eventually she laughs but it's a false and shabby effort.

'I … forgot … something.' Her mouth forms the words with effort.

I hide the book under the covers. I don't want to be ribbed again.

'Constance, I was wondering…' I wait for her to

make a witty retort as she usually does but there is nothing. I clear my throat. I don't like asking for things. It isn't in my nature. 'It's nothing really. But I wanted to look good... Just for once, you know? Or at least ... it's just ... I .... want ... to...'

It's like we are both learning to speak English again and if it wasn't for the humiliation of asking for something it'd be quite comical. I feel the colour rush my face.

I try again.

'Talking of dresses.' (Which we weren't.) 'I was wondering if I can borrow that blue velvet dress of yours? I won't need it for long. Just for a couple of hours. A few at most. I'll keep it clean and look after it I promise.'

She's going to say no. Why would she let me lend something as beautiful as that?

'Course you can.' Her words seem to come from far away and be placed in her mouth so that she isn't really connected to them. It'll do for me.

'You are the best friend ever.' I forget about holding the blanket around me and rush to give her a hug. Her arms hang limply at her sides.

'I'm so excited.' I let her go and leap over to

admire the dress, which is about the most exquisite piece of tailoring I have ever set eyes on. I am going to strut around the theatre in it making certain that everyone sees me. I might even wear it down to the docks so that Mabel can see me and die with jealousy. It will be brilliant to look halfway decent for once. I am so sick of looking like a half-drowned rat. Perhaps with this dress on I can feel beautiful. 'Thank you so, so, so, so, so, so much!'

I'm hooting for no apparent reason. Constance laughs too but it's that peculiar, strained version. It might be caused by my audacity in asking her to let me wear her dress or the near-to-nude state she found me in. I don't care. I'm riding the crest of a cloud of joy. For once I am winning.

'I'm just going to…' Constance turns and shuts the door gently behind her as she leaves. Another odd experience to add to all the others in my life of late.

I take the dress off its hanger as if it is something regal and almost blub at the softness of it. Spinning to see myself in the scratched looking glass, I jump up and down with excitement. I lie with it on top of me on my bed and let it fall majestically about me. Forgiving its scent of mothballs as it ripples down over my legs and fronds of it tickle my ankles. I am Cinderella going to the ball. I close my eyes. The theatre doesn't exist anymore. The dreary day has disappeared and I'm lulled into sleep. I see myself from above, pretty, with my eyes closed and the dress an ocean of calm. I'm made of water and for once I don't sink, I just let myself float in this gentlest, sensuous blue.

8

Part of this new and utterly un-thrilling Violet Night debacle is that I have to wait outside the theatre to see if the bereaved families turn up. So far none of them have. I've just used it as a chance to watch people.

Regular as clockwork the men climb their ladders to light the gaslights in the street.

'Come along, children. Forward march.' Mrs Crabtree, the governess, gives me her most sour and scathing expression as she marches past with her class of posh children in single file, like a well-behaved caterpillar, priggish the lot of them.

'Here you go, Nansi. Don't tell no one.' Adelaide from the sweet shop smuggles me a white mouse, which I will break in half and share with Bee later.

The street cleaners start to shovel as the traffic disperses. I watch the lights in the large round window of the Empire Theatre as they come to life and the large round moon vying for attention above them.

I have failed completely to stop Bee having to use the arsenic Sid provided her with to make Violet's stupid dress. She is now below stairs, lying in her crate, coughing and sweating. Her eyes are swollen and her breathing is laboured. I hate Sid so much right now I could kill him. I also hate myself for letting him do this to us.

Just as I have this thought, I see them. The very first people I stole from. There have been lots since. We are into double figures. And Sid has been in a rage, blaming me as if it's my fault that his heinous venture is failing. My body zings all over with adrenalin and nerves. I know it's wrong and all of it is fetid to its very core but waiting is so stupefyingly boring and in spite of myself I'm keen to see how Violet Night's act goes. She, of course, gets all her information through the obituaries and through bribes and spying. It's amazing how easily people pass on information if they are given the chance. They don't realise they are helping this scam, but as they never will I don't suppose it matters.

I hang back until the family in the crowd has

jostled to get into the theatre, then shove and elbow my way after them. I must get closer. Sweat trickles down into the small of my back. This is so wrong. So inexcusably wrong. And yet so thrilling.

I reach out my hand and drop it. The elder sister is looking straight at me but says nothing. She probably just wonders why I look so odd or perhaps she is still in shock. Mission accomplished, I push through the crowd, getting backstage, making sure I'm not seen or followed. I'm ashamed of myself for how much I'm enjoying all this.

I do my bit and tell George, one of the main boys, to find Sid and let him know to pull one of the usual turns. The plan is that Violet would go on after Con's magic act and before Imogen Lovell, the male impersonator. I want to make sure I have a really good view.

I go to the wings at the side of the stage and watch as Constance disappears from the magician's box to the largely underwhelmed response of the audience. They've seen it all before, they want something new and different. They are about to get it.

'El Pathetico' takes his bows to a smattering of applause and the announcements start for the next part of the show. Constance sees me and half waves then changes direction and disappears. She's acting so strangely. I must find out what I've done to upset her.

Scanning the stalls, I see the family. The sister looks happy which makes my skin burn with contempt at what we are about to do. It'll bring them comfort to think there is something beyond this life, I keep telling myself. It'll make them believe that Miranda is still with them. It's tripe but I'm willing to grasp at anything.

The announcer bangs his gavel on his podium like a judge pronouncing a sentence and it's time. Violet takes centre stage as if the theatre had been built with her in mind. A hush comes over the usually bawdy audience. People take matters of the spirits very seriously. They all want to be part of something unexplained.

Violet is certainly something to admire. Her green dress twinkles with tiny black beads which catch the light like miniscule dark stars. The limelight makes her face glow a ghoulish green-white. She shows no hint of nerves. I have to admit I'm impressed, however much I hate her. She has stage presence in bucket loads. You can't buy that sort of thing. You either have it or you don't. Mine would wither and die under this kind of pressure.

There are some stooges who've been trained up to pretend she is speaking to their late relatives in the audience. Kenneth, who is always hanging about asking Sid for a bit part in anything, has finally had his request granted. Audrey is also out there awaiting her big moment. She is at least seventy years old and has been with the theatre since the beginning of time, though no one is all that sure of what she does. Sid says she is his version of a theatre cat and jokes about her catching rats for breakfast. The real joke is that he doesn't need a cat to catch rats as he is already a snake.

'Welcome.' Violet has assumed a theatrical voice. It's deep and quivering with drama. I've heard the saying you can hear a pin drop but I don't think I've ever actually understood it until now. The audience is completely entranced. I'm sort of half mesmerised myself. 'I can only make contact with those who are open to the experience.'

There is a shift in the air as everyone tries to open their minds.

'I can only connect with those who are pure at heart so if you have committed a crime recently do not worry.'

There is a ripple of appreciative laughter from the audience, though there are a few guilty shuffles and straightening of jackets too.

'We shall begin now.'

Even though I know that what she is doing is absolute bunkum, I'm caught in its spell. She is a real professional. Closing her eyes she holds her fingers out in front of her as she feels the space for 'energies', as she calls it. Her energies draw her to Kenneth, who has definitely changed his mind about being involved as everybody's heads turn towards him.

'You have lost your mother…'

And on it goes. Kenneth only has to nod and look embarrassed and he does that with aplomb. Audrey has been told to be a bit more reluctant, then won over. Violet gives some supposedly private details about how she has a thing for a younger man, which she initially objects to and then starts to reveal that she was, indeed really is, in love with him, but fate had other plans for him and he was taken. I think she should win an award. Her acting is so much better than any of us expected. I always passed her off as old and hapless.

Violet is also cunning in the way she plays her part. Pretending she is shy to share the fabricated plot of Audrey's life with so big an audience. It's just perfect. And having set up the style and lured everyone into our net, we are on to the main act. I'm squirming but my pulse is quick. If we can pull this off it will be a brilliant *coup de théâtre*. Not that anyone will know I've had anything to do with it.

Violet goes for the girl rather than the parents. I knew she would. Maximum impact. I feel vomit rise in my throat.

'You.' The sister jumps out of her seat as if she has been given an electric shock. Violet makes sure that every single person in the audience is focused on her by making her stand, which she does defiantly, if shakily. She is hunched like a crow in her black get up. It's a pity the fashion is to stay so obviously in mourning or we could have used that as the first trick. 'I'm trying to ignore your mind but it is so crowded with thoughts and they are pushing their way out to me. Such sorrow. Such sorrow.' They could do with a bit of sad music here. I'll suggest it to Sid. Perhaps the unsettling tune from Bee's music box. 'You are thinking of a girl. The most beautiful girl. You are so sad.'

Violet keeps the audience ensorcelled as she details the dead girl's life. Guessing at the things the sisters used to do together. The audience are agog, as is the sister, but the final little cherry on the cake is about to come.

'She loved the sea, your sister, yes?'

The girl nods. Her face shines with astonishment and rapture.

'She is thinking of you. There is something in your pocket that will remind you of her. Look.'

The girl searches through her pocket. Eventually she pulls out a small segment of blue sea glass which she holds up to cries of shock from the onlookers. Lots of them won't have a clue what it is, even though it is all over the place on the mud flats of the docks. Violet realises this.

'It is glass that has been smoothed by the sea. She has given it to you as a sign that her love will always be there, as constant as the ocean. It is a present from the other side.'

Violet raises her hands to the heavens as the auditorium fills with gasps. The lights cut to black and with that she leaves the stage. I put my hand on my heart and thank my lucky stars that the girl didn't catch me dropping it in her pocket in the foyer earlier. Everyone loves the sea but there was that special link this time.

Violet takes her curtain call, so I bow in the wings and some of the stagehands think I'm just larking about so they clap for me. They're nice like that. I am exhilarated. We did it. We are a hit. I don't need to swim tonight unless I'm swimming in champagne.

My head is swirling when I get to the dressing room. I am part of a successful show. I want to get to my friends to see if they believed their eyes and ears or if they have suspicions about its authenticity.

Stripping off my dress, I put on Con's blue velvet one. She's said it's all right, so she won't mind if I have it for a few hours. There are some cornflower blue ribbons in a box of accessories. I tie a few of them in my hair in bows and then fasten a delphinium blue choker around my neck. I need to ride the excitement and enjoy myself, not put myself down as I'm so used to doing. I actually don't look half bad. I'm going to go down and see Bee and tell her all about it.

There's someone coming down the corridor outside, but I'm so wrapped up in myself I don't pay them any heed till they are right outside the door. By the time I recognise the voices it's almost too late. It's Sid for sure and I would rather die than let him see me in this outfit dreamily marvelling at myself and celebrating. He could cut me down with a single word.

For this reason, and perhaps some other sense of foreboding, I hide in the chest. I know it sounds preposterous but it's where I hide everything that is precious to me so it seems the obvious place. I've tried it for size before just in case of dire circumstances like this.

Constance is with Sid. I can hear her smoker's cough just outside the door. I hurry to fold myself in, crushing the dress and hoping that it won't leave marks in the material. With any luck their business down here will be over speedily and I can get on with my evening.

An unthinkable thought enters my head and I try to squeeze it out. I think they are going to have relations. That must be why Constance is so awkward when she sees me. She thinks I'll be disgusted and I will. Oh no! And I've shut myself in here so I'll be able to hear them canoodling. ARGH!

Opening my eyes wide against the darkness, I hear them come into the room and close the door behind them. Constance laughs her throaty, gravelly laugh. I try not to move a muscle. Should I spring out of the chest now and announce my presence with a 'Ta-dah!'? What would I say? I was just having a sleep in here? I was searching for something and managed to get myself trapped, but I suddenly realised that there wasn't a lock on the lid and I am only now opening it?

It's too late. The excruciating truth is that I'll just have to wait out whatever is going on with these two and then get out when they've gone. Please make it quick. Please.

In the womb of the trunk I hug my knees to my chest and pray I won't get cramp. It's a good job I'm used to hiding in small spaces. I can feel my borrowed books pressing into me comfortingly.

Sid's recognisable hiss is muffled but I can just make out what he's saying as it drips through the keyhole.

'Constance, my beauty.'

I quell the nausea at the image of his crooked smile. Sid thinks he is quite the lady's man.

'You can drop the act. We both know I've got you by the short and curlies.'

'Always witty. Always a strong word and a joke. That's what I admire in you, Constance, my sweet. Your spirit. Your pluck. You are quite magnificent, you know.'

Puke. This is an abominable thing to have to eavesdrop on.

'Thanks for the compliments, but let's get down to business.'

My stomach somersaults. I can't even put my fingers in my ears to block this out without making too much noise with them now so close. I consider again bursting out of the trunk and shouting 'Found it!' but that moment has passed and I bet it would be more than my life is worth. I wait for the sickening slurp of them kissing.

'I've found out what you're up to.' I hear the shake in Constance's speech though she is doing a good act of trying to hide it.

'Oh yes? And what is that, my dear?' Sid has put on his *I'm being nice* tone which he uses before he goes for the jugular.

'Don't pretend to me, Sid. I've seen her. I'd know that face anywhere.' There is a pause. I replay the words in my head and try to make some kind of sense from them. Nothing comes. 'It took me a while, granted, but as soon as it clicked…'

'I'm sure I don't know what you mean, my sweet.'

'Oh you know alright. I'll tell her if you like. I'll tell Nansi.'

Tell me? TELL ME WHAT? They have my complete attention.

'Ah, courageous indeed, but let us not forget who is actually in charge around here, Constance, there's a good girl.'

Perhaps Constance has taken me for someone else. Perhaps she has her own scam. If I'm supposed to be involved, I want to hear every detail so I can defend myself when the time comes.

'I've seen her mother. She's the spit of her.'

The air inside the trunk is sucked out. My head

95

swims. My skin reels with hot stabbing pains. I want to explode out of this box and rush at them. Scream at them, 'Where is she?' I clench my teeth so hard I almost pass out.

'And I can very easily tell Nansi where she is.'

Is. Is. IS. The word reverberates around me like a wasp intent on stinging. I can't feel my body anymore. Everything is still. The air, my heart, my blood. Everything.

Sid sits down heavily on the trunk. I know it's him from his recognisable sigh. 'What is it you want from me?'

Why isn't he asking her what she's talking about? Why isn't he threatening to send her to Bedlam for talking such utter rot?

'I want to be a star, Sid.'

There is no response. I think Constance takes this as a sign of acquiescence.

'I want to be top billing and I want my name out the front. I want a piece in the paper about how you plucked me from nowhere and recognised how famous I was going to be because of my talent.'

I can't comprehend anything. I'm numb and more alive than I've ever been at the same time.

Sid shifts his weight. I open my eyes wide as if that will help me hear them more clearly. Their voices are harder to hear now that Sid is blocking the keyhole with his leg and I'm having to concentrate so hard to pick up everything.

'And what is that talent, my dear?'

'I'll sing. Anyone can hold a tune. It's not about that and you know it. It's about the mirrors and the lights and the adoration. And the money.' She stops.

Just say where my mother is. SAY IT.

'If you don't put me there, I'll tell Nansi you lied to her all this time about her mother being missing. I'll tell her where her mother is. I'll tell her, Sid. Don't think I won't. You have my word on that.'

'Ah, and an actress's word is her bond.' He laughs a wheezing, cyanide snicker.

I'm screaming inside my head so loudly that I'm sure it must be coming out of my mouth.

'Her mother is dead.' Sid's words make my heart squeeze so hard I almost scream with agony. Why would Con make this up? What scam is she trying to pull?

He stands up and his voice comes through to me loud and clear. 'To me at least.'

The world swirls about me in navy sparkles. I am sucking to breathe.

'Where have you seen her?'

'Now that would be telling, and I can't be a tattle-tale.'

I am buried alive.

'Come on now, there's a good girl. I already know where she is but I want to see if you are telling me the truth.'

She is alive. She is alive. She is alive. I hear the horses gadding about on the street above, high heels pounding cobblestones, the colours are gleaming even in here, turquoise and blues, roses and orange, smells fill my nostrils, the dryness of dust, the tang of the thrilling air. I want to leap and yell, dance and fly. I've swelled to the size of the box with joy. My mother is alive. My mother is alive. The world tips back and I am in blackness but I am no longer alone.

There is a sudden shift against the box and I hear Constance screech.

'Please, Sid. Please. I promise. I was just trying my luck. Messing with you. I won't say anything. Honest I won't.'

I'm alert again. Constance is afraid. Very afraid.

'It's such a shame, Constance. You leave me with something of a problem.' Sid's voice is an icicle. Spiteful. I can imagine his sneering lip, the globules of saliva stretched in strings between his teeth as he speaks. 'I think you've become a danger to me.'

'I'm not, Sid. I promise I'm not. Listen, I'll move on. I'll leave. Today. I'll leave today. I'll go now. Right now. Just let me go. Please.' Her voice peters out.

'You see, if the others were to find out that you disobeyed me and I let you get away with it, then they might think I was going soft. I already let you get away with something, didn't I?'

'I don't know what you're talking about.'

I do. When Constance rolled her eyes at him. Sid never forgets a thing and he doesn't let anything slide.

There is a noise then which I can only describe as a silence so thick it is audible, then a thud breaks it and the pungent phosphorous smell of a match being struck.

'I apologise, Constance, but business is business.'

He leaves. The door shuts. I wait, my eyelids

stinging from staring into the darkness for so long. A tinny scent winds its way into the chest and tickles my gag reflex. Eventually I push the lid up, trying to keep my heartbeat in my throat, trying with all my might not to make a single sound. I know what will be there.

However petrifying the sight of Constance's lifeless body is, it's still second to the relief I feel that Sid has left. He's strangled her. I've heard of him being involved in things like this before, but I would never have believed it. He is like a father to me. The only father I've ever known.

Shock comes pouring in like a river. He has told me for as long as I can recall that my mother is missing and all that time he has known where she was. Perhaps she has been looking for me. Perhaps he has told her that I am dead. My legs give way beneath me.

Constance lies in front of me but I feel nothing for her. I feel only for my mother. My mother. I'm more angry than I've ever been. I want to shake her back to life. I want to shout at her. 'Where is my mother? Tell me. How could you? We were supposed to be friends.'

And immediately I realise we weren't really

friends. I didn't know her at all and she was willing to put ambition ahead of me. As well as the anger, I feel something akin to pity for her or at least I know I will one day.

I have got to leave here. This place I've called home. It is time to escape.

9

I shove my measly things into a carpetbag, but can't take the books which breaks my heart. I need to be light to run. I'll come back for them.

I give a quick goodbye to my room. I know it's just a cold little tomb but it's all I've known so I can't help getting choked up. Constance's body stops me. I unfreeze my brain enough to let in the intense horror of her death. A low keening moan reaches up from somewhere and I have to physically bite down on my hand to stop it.

Checking over my shoulder, I hasten along the corridor, terrified that Sid will come back for Constance's body and discover me. I need to get Bee and run.

She is flat out in her crate. I try to wake her but she is in so deep a sleep that all I can get is a flicker from her swollen eyelids before she tumbles back into dreams.

'Bee. You have to wake up. We have got to go.' I shake her. Her head lolls. 'Bee, please. Please wake up.'

There is no response. I try to lift her but she is a dead weight and I simply haven't got enough strength in my body.

'I'll come back for you. As soon as I can.'

I suppress a sob. I will sort this out and get her away from this place. But I need to get myself to safety first. I'll give a message to one of the stagehands to deliver to Bee when she wakes up. I have to let her know she hasn't been abandoned. They will all be up by the stage so I'm going to have to go there before I can escape.

Gassy Jack leans against a cut-out elephant at the side of the stage and picks at his teeth with a match. 'Going somewhere?' His bowler hat is entirely unbecoming.

'I'm just looking for someone. Not that it's any of your business.' The safety curtain is down and there are lots of people clearing the stage of the scenery from this evening's acts.

'Anyone in particular?' Gassy Jack comes closer so I can smell his festering breath. His efforts with the matchstick have failed completely and he has the remains of at least his last three meals plastered to his rancid teeth.

'No.' I haven't got the brainpower to come up with a witty retort. All my senses are panicked.

'Only someone's looking for you.'

My heart skips a beat. His eyes gleam. I know in that second that Gassy Jack is the one who will dispose of Con's body. He is the one who does the dirty work. I want to reach out and box him by the ears, but instead I turn on my heel and race across the stage, hurling into people as I pass, ignoring the swearing and shouts.

I almost tip forward as I skid to a stop. Sid is on the far side of the stage, coming towards me. He must have been looking for me to check whether I'd been down to the room and seen the body. If I'd played it cool I could have given him a blank expression and a fistful of lies about how I hadn't seen anything. There's no way I can come across as innocent now, I practically left burn marks on the boards I stopped so sharply.

Sid's face is so composed it is a death mask. Could I convince him to let me keep his secret and be another Gassy Jack? Or that I want to join him in his murderous ways and become a notorious outlaw or as famous as the Ripper? But he knows I struggle with making things fair and square. Thieving is one thing, murder quite another.

But maybe I would do it if he would tell me where *she* is. I would do anything.

Reading the thunderous dark in his eyes, I know that he has no intention of telling me the truth. Some things don't need to be spoken when you've spent enough time with someone. My hands clench and unclench. Sid is waiting to see what I will do. I look over my shoulder and see Gassy Jack walking towards me with unequivocally vicious intent. Sid slithers towards me from the other direction as if he is on castors. I've got to think fast.

Sid is in front of me, Gassy Jack behind. The safety curtain is iron so I can't get into the auditorium. I run pell-mell upstage and jump. Down into the hole left by the trap door, down underneath the stage.

My ankle twists painfully as I land, but the panic and lust for survival are too strong to give up now.

'I'm fine. I'm fine.' The two men who are about

to wind the trap back up into place are all over me with concern. I shrug them off roughly and limp away as quickly as I can, trying to plan my escape as I go. They make no move to follow me and soon they are hidden behind ropes and cogs and other stage paraphernalia.

It's dark down here and most of the backstage crew are either up on the boards or have gone home. They clear quickly after a show, wanting a sharp finish and a swift bevvy. Also, Sid never comes down here because it's dusty and dirty and for 'the peasants' as he calls them. So, it doesn't matter if they leave jobs half done, or completely undone, as he will never know.

Never till now, I think. He won't jump through the star trap because he will consider himself too dignified and he won't let Gassy Jack attract too much attention because once they catch me and kill me they won't want any questions.

Catch me and kill me. The words ring in my ears.

There is an entrance at the back of the theatre. I'm stumbling and knocking into things, which isn't clever as they'll be able to see which way I've gone. Veering left, I smash into a huge stack of boxes and watch them and their contents cascade to the floor. I've created a catastrophic path for them to follow. I quickly retrace my footsteps and avoid creating any more pandemonium in the other direction as I hide.

There's an old costume chest. It worked for me before and I'm in so much pain there's no way I can outrun them. I'm used to small spaces so folding myself down into it is easy. I try to block out the excruciating stab in my ankle and allow myself to feel pleased that I have won, for the moment at least. Either that or I've given him the perfect coffin to lock me in and put me beneath the ground. My breathing feels amplified by the leather of the trunk. It's so loud I am afraid that just my being alive will alert them to my whereabouts. I clutch my carpetbag to my body as if it is a talisman and wait.

I don't know how long I am in here before claustrophobia sets in. It's not something I'm prone to but once it takes me in its grip it is blinding. I almost feel that surrendering is better than this suffocating airless tomb. I put my mouth to a hole in the side of the chest and suck deeply, fighting to calm my lungs and slow the pace of my heart. I move my mouth from the hole and risk peering through.

They are there. Pernicious Sid is livid and Gassy Jack is frantically nodding. I don't know how I didn't hear them coming. I was too carried away by the horror and the pressing dark. I try to listen.

'You should have held her fast. Not let her go.' Sid is at his most dangerous. I almost feel sorry for Gassy Jack. He is without wit or looks or fortune. 'We find her. We find her now. We don't leave any loose ends. Understand?'

There is a silence where Gassy Jack either deliberates or wipes Sid's spittle from his face. He is a nasty piece of work, that's for sure, but he isn't a murderous maniac. He also isn't brave. 'We'll find her.'

'We'd better.' Sid clouts him hard with the metal tip of his cane. 'Go on then, before I feel the need to take my rage out on someone.'

Sid pushes Jack so hard he loses his balance and falls in a twisting motion, flailing in mid-air, landing with a slam on his knees and palms. He is so close to my hiding spot. Too close. His mouth is bleeding profusely. I can see him wipe at it with his sleeve. From back here, the hole in the chest frames his face perfectly.

And then the worst happens. He looks straight into it. His face completely fills the hole. He even crawls towards it to get a better view of me, cowering.

'What is it?' He's got Sid's attention.

That's it. I'm going to die. They are going to nail the lid shut and take me out of here at the witching hour with a couple of shovels and no one to mourn me or care where I've gone. My mother will never know. I will never get to hold her again. Tears run down my cheeks. I am so close to finding her and now it is over.

Jack just stares. Frozen, with his mouth agape as if he can't believe his luck at finding me. Looking into his eyes, I beg, but know it's no use.

A strange uncertain expression comes over his features before he shakes it away. He wipes more blood from his mouth and staggers to his feet.

'Nothing. Come on. Let's find her.' He stumbles off along my staged chaotic path.

'That's the first good idea you've had all day.' Sid struts after him, an arrogant circus master breaking the spirit of his lion.

I wait until they are completely out of sight, then out of sound, and then I wait some more before easing the lid up and heaving my weight on to my good foot.

Pressing my swollen ankle into the ground, I realise it's worse than I'd thought and getting worse with every passing second. Taking one of the costumes out of the trunk, I rip a strip of fabric from its hem. The material is ripe with age and neglect so it tears easily. I create a makeshift bandage and tie it tightly around my ankle. I'm wasting time. But I have no choice but to strap myself up if I'm to put any weight on it at all. I try it again, gingerly, but with increasing firmness. You will work, I tell it. Dead is worse than injured.

I hobble to the staircase upstairs. The backstage is a mystifying warren which I've always moaned about when trying to show new people around but now I am so thankful I could kiss the walls. I take one of the smaller, most unused corridors then retrace my limping footsteps again. That's what they will expect me to do. I can't be caught. The corridors are dark now that everyone has gone. The metal of the lights sigh as they give up their earlier heat and start to contract.

I can't outrun them. The element of surprise is all I have at my disposal. My intelligence will have to see me through.

I gather my thoughts as sharply as I can. I won't go through the backstage door or any of the windows at the back of the building; they will expect that. While I'm limping towards the foyer I am, in my mind, racing towards the stained glass rose window at the front of The Empire and throwing myself through it, smashing in diamond colours on to the street below. A beauty surrounded with twinkling glass like an angel caught by a rainbow. Or a writhing, lacerated scruff-bag covered with coloured glass. I'm going out of the front door.

With every speck of courage I can muster, I head through the foyer and into the gas-lit street. I have nowhere to go. I stagger in the shadows towards the castle, which looms high above the street, guarded by its eyeless stone figures. They are hollow and haunting in the dark. They have seen everything with their empty eyes and locked it deep away in the roots that grow beneath Cardiff.

I check over my shoulder. There doesn't seem

to be anyone following me but I keep to the darkest spots as much as I can. Bawdy crowds spill from the pubs singing and jostling. Men tend their horses snorting white steam into the starless black. As I get further from the theatre the people are sparse and the night is even darker. The sky, which was earlier filled with low clouds, has thickened and the moon hangs in a slice so thin it could be painted with one brushstroke.

I'm going to hide in Bute Park. I can hunker down there till morning, then convince someone to take pity on me and take me outside town where I can plot my next move. I'll decide what that will be when my head is clear. When the light brings a new day.

When I find my mother, I won't be afraid of hard work. I could be a maid for one of those grand houses out in the countryside, so I can support her if she hasn't means. I could send word for Bee and she could work there too. It wouldn't do for a lifetime but it might be nice to be sure what's expected of me, where I'm able to sleep at night after a hard day's work. Perhaps we could get the paddle steamer across the channel to England and start a fresh life there, leaving our ghosts behind us. Living as a family. A real and proper family.

Pure pain wracks my body from my ankle up. I need to take the weight off it as soon as possible. I'm feeling my way along the castle walls now. Grateful for the solid strength to prop me up. There are figures out there in the thick green dark. It's impossible to know whether Sid is one of them. I am stricken by panic again, but don't have time to indulge it.

Slipping into the castle grounds is easy enough. My eyes begin adjusting. I need to make my way up along the river as far as I can before I find somewhere to hide. The ground is uneven and no amount of imagining a happy future is enough to cover the pain any more. Wiping my forehead, I realise there is a very real chance that if I keep pushing forward I might end up unconscious, here on the open grass. Hiding has worked for me so far and the rustling bushes of the park seem to whisper that they will give me a safe place to rest. I can see the hulk of the castle holding up the night sky. I'll just rest here until very first light then try to convince one of the boat boys to take me down the river.

I freeze like a petrified hare. I'm not alone. Someone else is here. Searching, I can only make out the shapes I have seen before. The dark is so thick you could chew it. I could very well walk straight into someone if I carry on moving.

Standing stock still, I close my eyes to use my other senses and I know Sid is here with me. There's the sharp twang of cologne, the stink of his greasy skin and an indescribable noise that always announces his presence. Somewhere between a hiss and a sniff.

He is so close that I could put my hands out and touch him. I stay still. More still than I've ever been. Holding my breath, keeping my eyes squeezed tight shut, feeling my pulse slow with the lack of oxygen. He is moving away, I'm sure of it. That sickening smell is lessening. The sound in the air has given way to the rap of my own blood against my veins.

Someone grips my arm. I should know never to trust my senses.

'What do you want?' I surprise myself with the strength in my voice. If I'm going to die I'm not going out as a coward.

'Nansi.' It's Sid alright.

There is a shuffle close to him and a match struck. Gassy Jack's face appears above a hand-held lantern. He looks scared as hell.

'Yes, it's me.' There is a rage building in my bones and it's burning away any common sense I ever had. 'And who are you, Sid? Not the father you pretended to be. You're a liar. A liar and a murderer.'

He seems taken aback by my reaction. He probably expected me to drop to my knees and beg for my life, but I'm done with being walked over all the time and I can't control my temper anymore. It sparks out of me in flames.

'Your real father left your mother clawing to me for mercy.'

'Where is she?' I don't need to make it any clearer. He knows who I mean. 'Where is my mother?'

My voice cracks on the last word. My life has been a lie. Everything has been vicious lie, after rotten lie, after stinking dirty lie.

'Ah. I'm afraid she had to go elsewhere so that I could look after you.'

'What did you do?' I can feel hatred rippling through me. Flexing every muscle, stinging every nerve.

'Now wouldn't you like to know.' He laughs at this and my blood runs cold. He isn't human. He can't be. 'I'm afraid I can't give you that information right now. You see, I can't be convinced you'll co-operate and I've worked too hard for things to give in now.'

'I'll find her. She'll come back for me.'

'But I'm afraid she isn't capable of going anywhere. She's a little tied up.'

'Where is my mother?' I scream this bit.

The sky is a swirling ink. A gull swoops low and white, spectral against the navy dark. I'm losing my grip.

'I'm not going to tell you, so shut your mouth.'

'You made me a slave.' I have never felt such malice. 'I will find her. I'll tell her what you did. We'll go to the police together and tell them and they'll lock you up or have you hanged.'

'Don't be pathetic, dear girl. You can't remember anything. She could walk right past you and you wouldn't know her.'

'I remember her. She was beautiful. And she is the spit of me.' I don't know this for sure but I'm clinging to Constance's words. 'And she loved me.'

He laughs again. I feel something crack in my throat but I won't cry. Not for him. I'll never show weakness again.

'I'm left with something of a dilemma. You've become a bit of a fly in the ointment and you know how I like my plans to run smoothly.'

I don't know what he's talking about. I am filled up with hate and it's pushing outwards against my skin, trying to break through.

'I'm afraid you may be made of stronger stuff than I had given you credit for. What to do, eh, Jack? Life can be such a bore sometimes.'

I can see how much Gassy Jack is quaking from the unsteady flicker of the candle.

The flames from the lamp dance about Sid's face and I see him as he is. The very devil. Evil to the core and without hope of changing.

Suddenly it's more than I can stand. I let out a bloodcurdling scream and rush at him, shoving, battling, thumping, screaming. It's a short attack because my frenzy is halted abruptly by a whack to the back of my skull. I stop in surprise. The world is a glimmering, glowing magic lantern show. I feel the thud as Sid brings his cane down on my forehead this time and my legs give way beneath me. I look up at Sid and Gassy Jack, whose lamp is trembling so badly.

'Finish it.' Sid nods to Jack.

I will not cry. I am filled with hate and nothing more. There is blood on my tongue, meaty and hot.

He tries again to give the cane to Jack but Jack's hands hang limply at his sides, the lamp now knocking against his knees. He's in shock. For all his bravado he is just a boy.

'Where is my mother?' It's hard to speak. My teeth are soft and my head is a baby's rattle.

I feel another blow to the top of my head and another. Then there is nothing but white.

I'm being dragged by my feet. I can taste wet grass, mud, metal and I hear a high-pitched screech which might be me, I'm not sure. Above that I can hear Jack crying. He is no doubt paying for not doing his job properly. The water is close now. Waiting. It knows it is about to take me in again. How funny that just as I find out my mother is alive I am going to die. The water laughs at this. We've always been friends.

My hands are taken now and I'm lifted. I feel

weightless. It's like swimming. I fly through the air.

As I hit the river, reality slaps me hard. My mother. She is in this life somewhere. I can't die. I have to find her.

The water is a thousand slicing cuts. I gasp against it as it fills my mouth. It drags me, gurgles me downwards, pulls me down, down to the bottom, into the earth, down, and then there is a tug inside and I am swimming. Up towards the surface and back towards revenge. I will not be beaten. Not this day. Not ever. I use the surge of the water to carry me downstream. I fill my lungs with air to help me float then, when the current becomes less strong, I put all my energy into saving my life.

I reach the sludge of the far side and crawl my way up it. Yelping with the pain and cold. I check behind me.

It was Gassy Jack who threw me in the water. He has mocked me enough times about my love of swimming. He wanted to give me a tiny chance at life. Sid would never have left a loose end.

Like I said before, it's hard to drown if you are me.

10

My vision is hazy when I start to come round and I have to blink several times to see where I am. I try to move but it hurts all over.

'Don't move.'

Blinking hard, I see that I am surrounded by the mudlarks from the docks.

'You're not dead then?' It's the boy who threw me the bread roll. I search my brain for his name. Dylan. That's it.

A few of them chuckle. They are huddled around a tiny fire. It's smoky and the air is heavy and choking.

'I don't think so.' My lips feel dry and cracked but I just about manage a smile. I know I am in good company with this lot.

'How are you feeling?'

I am feeling lots of things. Dazed. Confused. Angry. Excited. In the end I go with, 'Sore.'

They hoot with laughter at that.

'Here. Take this.' He hands me a bottle of something that smells like poison. 'It's brandy. Get it down you before I change my mind and drink it myself.'

Hesitantly I take a sip. It burns my lips, sends flames down my gullet and my stomach makes a huge rumbling sound. 'That's disgusting.'

'Suit yourself.' He takes it back and necks a huge glug.

'Where am I?' I kind of recognise the place, or feel as if I should, but my brain isn't functioning normally yet.

'Don't try to speak if it hurts, you idiot,' he jibes, then winks and takes another slug. 'You're in the tunnel. It's a handy place to hide out.'

I look around me and realise that of course that's where we are. Everything is green and cream tiles. Clean and polished new. The scent of the sea laces the smoke and I feel the river pounding above our heads.

'We are making the most of it before they finish it, aren't we lads?'

He gets a cheer from the other boys.

'Oy, Dylan. Don't forget about the girls.'

I recognise that voice. It's Mabel Jones. I wonder what she's doing here and if she's about to say something catty as she usually does. She comes over to me to speak. 'You're safe here. Sid doesn't know where you are.'

If I had the energy my eyes would gawk out on sticks. I forget how rife gossip is in the docks.

Dylan puts his arm around Mabel and she pretends to shrug it off. 'Mabel saw you climb up the bank. She came to get us so we could bring you here and make you safe.'

'I'm not so bad after all now, am I?' She takes Dylan's brandy and has a swig without reacting. I guess she's more used to drinking it than I am. She has a huge red mark up her cheek. I wonder if her mother has given her a beating again.

'Thank you.' I mean it too. I try to let her know that with two words.

'Just don't expect me to be nice all the time is all.'

She gives me her usual nasty stare then takes the arm of a girl who can be no more than seven, and walks off down the tunnel with her. I can hear her start telling a story about a girl who went off to an island far away and made up all her own rules. I'm guessing from the way she speaks to the girl that she is her little sister. I think I can understand why Mabel is so prickly all the time. I need to try harder to be nice. But not to everyone.

I think of Sid and it feels as if someone has tightened a belt around my head and is pulling hard. Tears well up in my eyes but I won't shed them. I have to be strong and make a plan. I am not alone in this world, as I had been led to believe. My anger threatens to consume me again but I need to use it properly.

I test out my body. My head feels as if someone has sawed the top of it off and exposed my brain to the air. It's excruciating. The part of my face where Sid hit me with his cane is swollen and sore and even though it is dark I can see my cheekbone in my peripheral vision, which is strange. I am covered with a thick woollen blanket so I can't see my ankle, but I know it is bad as I can't move it an inch without pain. The rest of my body aches and twinges but it feels as if I will recover.

I am fortunate to be here at all. By rights I should have been swept away by the current to the sea. I know that I am stronger than the water now. The clang of church bells echo through the tunnel.

'That's it, you lot.' One of the tunnel miners has turned up for a day's digging. 'Out you go.'

He has a kindly face and he worried when he sees me. 'Dear Lord. This one needs a doctor.'

'I'll be fine, thank you.' I can't risk seeing a doctor. What if Sid gets word of it? What if he knows I'm still alive? I try to get up but the pain is excruciating and I cry out before I can stop myself.

'I should report you lot to the coppers.' The man with the kind face shakes his head at me and the mudlarks who are collecting up their things. 'Take this. But bring it back later. You hear me?'

He pushes a cart towards us and I am hoisted in and wheeled outside. The pain is too much but having these people be so kind to me makes me manage it. They keep forcing tots of brandy on me and even though I hate the taste it does start to numb my body so I can relax.

'Where do you want to be taken, M'lady?'

That's Dylan pretending to be posh and I want to laugh but I'm afraid I'll crumple.

'I don't have anywhere to go.'

We come out into the early dawn of Tiger Bay. The sun is rising in a rose pink glow this morning. I may be broken but it is beautiful and I feel it deep inside. A new day is here and I have a new life because now I have hope.

'Give us a minute.'

Most of the mudlarks have scattered already but a few are still hanging about and Dylan huddles with them in a circle. They are obviously talking about me because they look over their shoulders every now and again. Eventually they turn to me to share their plan.

'There's a ship. Jimmy is working on it.' Dylan is obviously the spokesperson for this bunch. A boy who I guess must be Jimmy stands forward and looks proud of himself. 'It's docked for a few weeks. Storm damage. Lots of holes in the keel and bow.'

'It's a wonder it's still floating with Jimmy working on it,' one of the girls shouts and then runs off in a flurry of shawls and laughter.

'We can hide you there for a bit. While you get better?' You can see they are all proud of their idea.

'There's a room where we keep our stuff. No one will tell on you cos I'm in charge, see?' Jimmy's chest swells with pride as he says this.

'It sounds perfect.' It really does. I need somewhere to sleep and gather my strength. 'But I need to save Bee and get my things and...'

My head spins and I can't think straight.

They take over then. I'm wheeled to the ship and carried up the gangplank with kindly hands under my arms and feet. I can see its masts cutting the orange pink sky above the crow's nest, the wind teasing the sails, birds preening themselves on the rigging. I'm carried down into a cabin below deck and placed on a bunk, while Jimmy collects the tools his team will need and leaves me there with a swaying glass of water at my side. It smells of oil and wood in here but my berth is warm and safe and the gentle rock of the waves beneath me drifts me into sleep.

I don't know how long I slept but I feel dazed and sick. The ship, which has sucked and reeled beneath me in my nightmares, is swaying very gently and there are comforting creaks all around. There is a breeze from somewhere and it carries the sounds of the outside in. I can hear horses and carts, conversation and footsteps, the slide and lap of the water against the dock wall and against the hull. Someone is humming a tune. I blink hard against the pain in my temples and open my eyes, squinting.

'Nansi!' It's Bee. She rushes at me as if she is going to hug me, then stops short as she realises that it would probably hurt me.

'Bee!' I pull her to me anyway, wincing at the pain but so relieved to see her that it's worth it. 'How did you know where I was?'

'The mudlarks told me.' She is beaming. 'Don't worry. No one else knows.'

I feel a judder of fear as I think of Sid. It quickly turns to fury.

'I can't stay long. I have to get back. I have to…'

Bee starts coughing and once she starts she can't stop. She bangs her chest with her fist and then holds a piece of cloth to her mouth. She tries to hide it but I can see that it is streaked with blood.

'How long have you been ill?' When I take her in properly she looks sickly, with huge dark wells under her eyes and dry patches all over her skin. Her hair, which usually shoots straight out from her head, is limp and frazzled.

'I'm fine. It's just a cold.' She is always brave. It's one of the many things I love about her.

'It's since you made that dress, isn't it?' I try not to let the cold hatred bleed out in my voice but the air turns sour anyway.

'I brought you these.'

My books. My books. My books. I clutch them to me with such joy I'm afraid they may be pulped by the force of my love. I lay them out on my chrysalis of blankets and run my fingers over their covers, feeling the indents of the lettering, the comfort of their familiarity on my skin. I know they aren't mine really, and I will return them one day, but for now they are a light when everything else is dark.

'Bee. There's something I have to tell you.' I don't know how to tell her everything but I have to start somewhere and I need to get it out like pus from an infected scab.

'Sid killed Constance.' Blurting it out brings all the shock back. 'He throttled her. She's dead. I saw her body.'

'He said she went away.' Bee looks utterly horrified. Perhaps she trusted him as I did. Once.

'I saw her. With my own two eyes. Believe me.'

She nods solemnly.

'He chased me. Him and Gassy Jack. He did

this to me and then Jack threw me in the river to drown. He is more evil than we thought. I mean I knew…' My voice collapses but I bring it back. 'My mother is alive, Bee.' The icicle in my throat threatens to stab its way out. 'She is alive and I am going to find her. And when I find her we will go away from all this. Do you hear me?'

Her eyes are saucers. I think she fears I am suffering with delirium.

'I don't know where she is but I intend to find her. Sid has been keeping her from me.' I pause to let everything sink in. 'He thinks I am dead now?'

She nods again.

'Then we have that on our side.'

I pat the bed beside me and stack the books in a pile against me so there is room for her to sit. 'Life is going to be different, Bee. I promise you.'

I hold her close to me. I can tell from the stains on her fingertips that there has been more than one Violet Night dress.

Between nightmares and dreams, I have been hatching a plan to get me into that theatre, so I can find out where my mother is somehow. I need to build my strength up.

We huddle down together in that gently

swaying room and read the story of 'The Snow Queen'. Snowflakes dance around us in fluttering white wings. Bee reads slowly, sounding out each word. When we are in the grip of the story she asks me to take over so we can find out what happens more quickly. I read how the Robber Girl helps Gerda to escape and as she rushes towards the Northern Lights on the back of a reindeer, the ice inside me starts to thaw and the world is filled with light and possibility. The Robber Girl can change her ways and become good and I will do the same. I will be the girl I was always meant to be. As I turn the pages I imagine writing the story of my own life and how it will change with each new chapter.

11

We are into October now. The cloying wasp-thick hours of early autumn are over and winter prepares itself with crisp efficiency. The rock and tilt of the ship has cradled me for long enough and it, like me, has recovered and is due to set sail soon.

Because the days are shorter and darker the theatre will be busier. This has been factored into our plan. Bee brings me news of the theatre whenever she can. Violet Night is still there, of course, demanding ever more extreme costumes, making Bee more and more ill by the day. They have been rehearsing for *Aladdin*. Sid has taken to the stage himself now that he has found the perfect part and is playing the Evil Uncle Abanazar, which I'm certain suits him.

I am trying out my disguise. At first I keep to the shadows if I see anyone I know, but as I get braver I hide less, and eventually I feel bold and carefree in this get-up. I can enjoy the familiar hustle and shove of life and wonder at how freeing it is to be dressed as a boy.

'Good day to you.' I'm trying out my boy's voice. It's still a bit squeaky and the girl I speak to pulls a face. My wig is cropped and brown. The trousers make me walk in a different way.

'Hullo to you.' This time I get a hullo back and no weird face, so my disguise must be improving. I do a little heel kick for joy then break into a sprint. I'm wearing no restrictive undergarments. I can run about without anyone taking even a tiny bit of notice. It's wonderful. I shall have a go on a bicycle if I can get my hands on one.

Bee has been telling me how things have changed at the theatre while I have been recovering. It's strange to talk about how that world has moved on without me in it. Gassy Jack has disappeared, probably dead. That will be Sid, covering his traces so nobody can tell about Con. I'm not surprised but I am so sad. Without him, I wouldn't even be here. He was braver than I gave him credit for. And if Sid has done for Jack, nobody will investigate. There are lots of people who work and live without any documents in that theatre. I should know. I was one of them. As far as the world is concerned I don't exist.

I am well. My ankle no longer pains me. My face is bruised but they've faded to dull yellows and greys. I have a scar that runs the length of my cheek, an ugly, raised seam as if I have been stitched together, but I must be thankful that I kept my sight.

Tonight is the opening night of the extravaganza *Aladdin* and so Sid is guaranteed to be out of his office on stage at least some of the time. Bee will be watching in the wings to warn me if anything goes awry.

I will buy myself some trousers if I survive this. If I get through this, I'm going to do all sorts of things that people will call 'advanced'. I might even get my hair chopped off. If I can make it through without being murdered I will do whatever I want for the rest of my life. I hope my mother won't mind. I'll bet she is for women's suffrage. I'll bet she is just marvellous in every way imaginable.

I'm terrified and at the point of tears, but I don't want to draw attention to myself. Also, I won't waste another tear on Sid. Not one, ever again.

Concentrating on the plan is the only way forward.

Where is my mother? I imagine her onstage being adored by thousands of people. I imagine her in the darkness of a cellar, sewing by the light of a small oil lamp till her fingers bleed and her eyes tear. I imagine her having another family, a husband who loves her, a child who she loves more than she ever loved me. I imagine her dying before she ever knows that I am still here. Dying before I have a chance to find her. It spurs me on.

There are so many theatregoers making their way into the Empire. I stand across the street watching them in their finery, chatting and buzzing with happiness and excitement. Violet Night is big news and has brought people from far and wide. Of course this fame and fortune will be short-lived as the audiences are easily bored, so Sid is making the most of it while he can. Bee told me that he doesn't even bother with real bereaved families anymore. It's easier and more reliable just to get stooges. That way she can be on every night. I can see a poster of her with chopsticks in her hair from the doorway I'm hiding in. It looks as though ticket sales are soaring. The lamplighters have finished their work and the streets glow, fizzle and pop.

Being a thief has given me the gift of passing by unnoticed. There will be hours of entertainment on the bill, which means a consistent stream of people coming in and out. I am relying on the chaos to keep Sid busy. He won't be able to resist basking in the admiration of the crowd.

I sneak to the back of the theatre. It's easy enough in this early dark. There aren't many lamps lit back here. I know this place like the back of my hand so I find the window easily enough. The catches on it aren't that smart and I've cracked them on other people's houses enough times in the past to get in without causing too much damage. Bee offered to open the window for me but I didn't want her to get caught. It's just not worth the risk when breaking in is so easy for me.

It feels so hostile to me now. This place I called home for so many years. I see the backstage area for what it really is. Dirty, unloved, uncared for, cheap. Sid cuts back where his beloved audience can't see. Avoiding my room completely, I creep along the corridors, using the ones least travelled, all my senses sharp.

The extravaganza is reported to be spectacular. It takes a lot of people to make that happen. The lime boys will be there trying out their new spotlights. Stagehands will be pulling pieces of scenery across the stage and flying things and people in from the rafters. All the performers and dancers will be involved, either on stage or in helping others with quick costume changes. Bee tells me that there is a scene in a palace where the whole harem of dancers surround Uncle Abanazar and even some of the men are on stage in yashmaks, doing a belly dance, to swell the crowd. This will be our best chance but we have had to time it perfectly.

Sid's office is close enough to the stage that I can hear the 'boos' and 'hisses' of the audience. I try the doorknob in the hope of a miracle but it is locked. Taking a hairpin from my pocket, I bend it to a usable shape. My hands are trembling and my mouth is dry as an old bone, but I grit my teeth and concentrate. I push the pin into the keyhole and jiggle it about, waiting for the click as the lock is released. It doesn't come. The roar of laughter from the audience makes me fumble and drop the pin and I have to crawl about on the floor to find it.

I see it eventually and wipe my hands down my trousers so that I can pick it up and try again.

'Come on. Come on, please.'

I jab it into the lock and will it to work. It clicks.

'Thank you.'

I check about me. The band strikes up an oriental tune and Sid's voice bellows out a song. He isn't a singer but the villain can always get away with being fairly useless. I wish I could watch him so I could jeer at him. The song will only last about three minutes and then he is offstage until the second half. Long enough to come to his office and catch me red-handed. I let myself in and close the door quietly behind me.

It's the same as always. That citrusy, acidic tang of his cologne. So much plusher than anywhere else that isn't open to the audience. Sid reasoning that he brings clients here to woo them so it has to be attractive. I see through that now. The gaslight hisses and pops as I turn up the jet. I need to move quickly.

The music is muffled now I've closed the door and panic is fuddling my thoughts.

'Concentrate.'

I wish I knew what I was looking for. There is a

bureau in the far corner. I pull the top towards me on its hinge and search through its contents, finding nothing useful at all. I look about me in exasperation. The desk. The top drawer. He always keeps that locked. My hands are shaking so violently that I have to stop and press them into the leather on top of the desk to calm myself.

'You can do this.'

I take the bent hairpin from my pocket and straighten it a little with my teeth then wriggle it into the lock and listen carefully until I feel it give. This has got to be it. Please. Please. I ease the drawer open on well-greased castors and lick the sweat from my top lip. The band is playing and Sid's muffled attempt at song can still be heard.

I move a silver hip flask from on top of a pile of papers, being careful not to leave a fingerprint on it. There are his accounts. I don't have time to look through them, though I'm betting they make interesting reading. It doesn't matter how successful Sid appears to be, he never has any money. Perhaps he is spending it on the horses or drinking it away. I place his latest account book to the right of the flask so that I remember the order to put them back in. There is an ink stamp and pad and a receipt book which shows that Sid spends lots of the theatre money on champagne and at the barbers.

At the bottom of the drawer I find a bundle of letters held together with string. I manage to untie the knot, though my heart is pounding so badly that it jerks my fingers. The first envelope contains a likeness of Sid's mother and a notification that she has died from the Angelton Asylum. I swallow the vile taste this brings to my mouth. The second is a demand for money from a solicitor as is the third, fourth and fifth. I am losing hope now. I open the sixth. It is again from Angelton Asylum and I am about to discard it when I notice that it has a different name on it. I can't quite make it out because it has been stained with water, or champagne, and the ink has run. It definitely doesn't begin with an 'A'. So it can't be Agnes, his mother. Who is this woman? Did Sid have someone else put in the asylum too? That evil, awful man. I go to put the letter back in the envelope and see that there is something else in there. It has stuck to the inside of the gum so I gently prise it off, being very careful not to tear it.

The woman in the photograph is my mother. She is exactly as I remember her. Exactly.

He has had her incarcerated in the asylum. Far away from Cardiff. This is how he deals with women who cross him. I don't know what she has done to make him do this, but I'm certain that's what has happened. He has threatened me with the asylum often enough.

The audience is quiet. I don't have time to leave. I hold the photograph of my mother to my lips for a second then put everything back in the drawer exactly as it was as speedily as possible. I frantically sweep the room for a hiding place. Turning the gaslights down, I crawl beneath his desk, holding my rattling breath tightly inside my chest. My thoughts scream at me: 'I didn't lock the drawer. I didn't lock the drawer.'

Sid comes in and turns the gas jets up. The lights spring into life. I sink into the floorboards as best I can and close my eyes, then open them again so I can best defend myself. Why didn't Bee come to let me know he was finished on stage? Why didn't I notice that the audience wasn't jeering anymore? I press my fingernails into my palms. His pointed Abanazar shoes appear. This would be comical if I wasn't facing death. My stomach cramps.

My mother. I must think of her. I know where she is. This is the moment I've been waiting for so long. I think of her locked up in a padded cell and a scream almost pushes out of my mouth. I bite my lip harder. I mustn't panic.

He goes to the closet where he keeps his changes of clothes, muttering beneath his breath. I can't make out what he's saying but I catch the odd expletive and I know he is annoyed about something. Good. He hangs something up then shuffles back to the desk. I can see up as far as his shins now. He is wearing trousers made of a gold shiny material. I can make out every sequin on them. If he drops something he will bend to pick it up and see me. I can't breathe. I can hear him moving things about above my head, shuffling papers and then the worst happens.

A pencil rolls from his desk and lands at his feet about an inch away from me. I will have to fight him. I will have to actually attack him, bowl him over in surprise, otherwise he will murder me for sure. I try to make myself even smaller as if I can melt into nothingness like a magician's assistant in a magical box.

Sid is so close his feet are only inches away. He

feels the underneath of the desk, just centimetres from where my head is. I watch his fingers scurrying along and brace myself to fight. They stop on a tiny brass skeleton key which is hanging from the underside of the desk on a hidden hook. It's for the drawer. Why didn't I think to look for a key? I could never have realised he would leave it in such an obvious place. He picks it off and immediately drops it within two inches of where I am crouched. I am going to die.

As if by magic, another set of feet appear.

'I'll get that for you, Sid.' It's Bee.

She gets a high-pitched scream in response, which in any other situation would be funny.

'Where the…? How many times have I told you not to sneak up on me like that?'

His rage takes his attention away from the desk and when Bee bends to get the key I know that this was her intention. She catches my eye for a second and then moves away. Clever, invisible Bee.

'What do you want?' He utters a series of uncouth words as she takes the key over to him.

'The first review is here already. I thought you'd want to know is all. But don't worry if you are too busy.'

'No. No. I'm not too busy at all. Where is it?' He is so predictable, the pathetic, slimy snake.

It isn't unheard of for a critic to dash off a review as he watches the show these days and someone always manages to get their hands on it before the curtain's down. Often the critic will be bribed into rewriting a bad review before it goes to print. Or they will sell a good one to the theatre manager if they can get a good price. Sometimes they are already in some kind of deal with the theatre.

'He's taken it off to the printers. I can tell you what it says. The beginning anyway. I read it myself.'

'Don't be ridiculous. You can't read.'

'I can.' Bee picks up a leaflet from the shelf. 'Rimmel's Toilet Vinegar. A tonic and refreshing. Lotion for the toilet and bath.'

Clever, clever Bee.

'Out of my way, you imbecile.'

Bee yelps. I assume Sid has pushed her aside. Then the door closes.

I wait for any noise or trickery. There is nothing but the sound of the piped gas and the tick, tock, ting of the clock. I move as quietly as a dormouse to a position where I can peer around the desk. Then take about an hour to actually look for fear that they'll both be standing there, Sid with his hand over Bee's mouth to stop her yelling out to warn me.

They have gone. The door to the office is shut. I swallow hard with relief and though my knees are quaking I pull myself together as best I can.

I can hear a ripple of laughter and a plinky plonky high-pitched tune played on the piano. There is the sound of an explosion – Sid has clearly splashed out on pyrotechnics this year – and an enthusiastic 'Boo!' from the crowd. I am safe. I open the door a crack. The corridor is empty.

I should go through backstage the way I came. Out through the window and into the safety of the dark at the back of the theatre, but if Sid is onstage then there is a quicker way. I tug my wig straight and taking up the stance of a boy again, head for the foyer doors.

The backstage is so dimly lit (so that Sid can save money) that the lights in the foyer make me blink. I pray that I won't bump into anyone I know. It's such a small walk to the open air but it feels as if I have a mountain to cross. The noise of the audience is louder here and one of the usherettes is standing in the doorway to the auditorium holding it open so that the stage can be seen. I can't help myself looking, just for a second.

Sid is rubbing a lamp way above Aladdin's head. Aladdin is a girl I've never seen before. She is cowering on the stage and begging for the lamp back. Sid has his eyes and eyebrows pencilled in to make them look darker and a huge dark velvet cloak. His hair has been slicked to his skull and his eyes gleam in the limelight like a demon's. He prefers lime to the new electric lamps as they make his teeth glitter more. There is a waterfall behind him with real water and a real donkey onstage. The drum rumbles as Sid conjures a spell and as the cymbals crash the stage is plunged into darkness and the girl playing Aladdin is left in the spotlight alone. The audience laughs as the donkey brays, presumably frightened by the noise.

'Are you alright there?'

My heart almost leaps from my mouth. It's Edith, the ticket seller, who was always a good friend to me. I can't let her see me, so I turn away brusquely and making my voice deeper reply, 'None of your beeswax.' Then make for the street outside.

She hollers after me, 'Charming. Nobody don't got no manners nowadays.'

The night is purple outside and threaded with diamond stars. I shove my hands in my pockets as a boy might and walk with my head down till I am out of sight of the theatre, expecting at every moment that Sid will grab me from behind. Once I am at a safe distance I throw my head back and howl a noise of overwhelming, all-encompassing joy to the sky.

I know where my mother is.

I want to shout these words out loud but I can't so I just howl again and again. Sending seagulls into mewing flight. Letting my voice weave through the turrets of the far-off Castle Coch. Flapping the pages of the books on the shelves of Cardiff free library and bowing the trees in the Hayes. My voice whooshes through the tunnel and breaks through the other side to Penarth. It sweeps back to me, clattering the copper pans which hang in the indoor market. Spinning the spools of bright thread and making the ribbons stream. The stained glass figures on St John's Church window dance to hear my happiness and the pipe organ blows rich chocolate notes to accompany them. I am the galloping white horse at the tip of a wave. I am the shimmering aqua green surf.

These wild thoughts get me across town and down to the docks. And then I stop, silent as a statue.

I should have locked the drawer.

12

I am lucky that Sid didn't notice the locket I kept back from the chest I stole for him. I've pawned it and have just enough money for the fare to Bridgend. I have never travelled by train before and am a little apprehensive but what awaits me at the other end is worth every jangling nerve and worry.

It's no wonder Sid has always discouraged me from leaving Cardiff. He was afraid that I might look elsewhere for my mother. He always warned me against the dangers of travel: tricksters, monsters, people who prey upon the innocent. And I fell for it. Hook, line and sinker.

It was easy enough to purchase my tickets and I'm now waiting on the platform with a suitcase in my hand and a flutter of fear in my stomach.

What will she be like when I find her? Will she remember me? What kind of health will she be in? I think of all the horrible things that happen to women in asylums and immediately try not to think about them.

'I am coming, Mother. Just hold on.'

I think I must have said that out loud because a young girl looks up at me warily and backs into her nanny's skirts. I smile and move further down the platform. I'm dressed as a boy again though I will change my clothes at the other side. As this costume worked before, I feel fairly confident in it and have mastered the art of walking and talking like a boy. I think I'm less likely to be preyed on by the conmen and women Sid warned me about dressing like this. It's funny really as he is the biggest conman of them all.

Despite my disguise I check the platform regularly as if I have a twitch. I've been standing here for an age now, having arrived early to make sure I didn't miss the train. Dylan the mudlark has drawn a map for me so I know where to go when I arrive. He didn't ask me why I needed it. Some people are good like that.

I hear the tug and clatter and the high-pitched squeal of the train before I see it. The platform is engulfed in steam as it draws to a stop. Billowing clouds silhouette everyone. I can still see the woman with the child in the swirling white and then, close behind them, the shape of a top hat. Fear swells inside me like a balloon about to burst. My heart echoes the tap, tap, tap of the man's cane on the platform.

I am dressed as a boy. It will be fine. Sid won't know it is me.

Tap, tap, tap.

Just stay still. Don't run. Don't draw any suspicion.

Tap, tap, tap.

Just don't look at him.

And then, of course, I do look. The man is close to me and he has grey hair and a huge bushy beard and chuckling lime-green eyes. It isn't Sid. Relief blasts out of my mouth and mixes with the steam.

'Are you getting on this train, boy?'

The porter leans out of the window frowning at me. I give a curt affirmation, which is unfair of me, but I can't trust my voice.

'Best get on then.'

He opens the door for me, which is kind and also lucky as I've never done it before. You slide the window down and then turn the handle on the outside. I nod again but try to make it less curt this time and hop up into the carriage. The door clanks behind me. I stow my small case above my head and sit on the hard bench. The nanny with the fearful child looks in, then seeing me thinks better of it and carries on to seek out a less peculiar passenger to travel with. I have space to breathe.

The train screams, a whistle sounds and chuffs of steam begin to cloud past the window. There is an almighty jerk and we are moving. Out of Cardiff and towards a new beginning. I lean back and close my eyes to quell my nausea. I've come this far. I can do this. I will do this.

I watch the town buildings give way to fields and hills in the distance. Trees and country houses and cattle. I wonder what kind of lives people must have out here, away from the hustle and swarm of the busy streets. I close my eyes and try to rest but it's impossible with all these thoughts buzzing against my skull so I give it up and watch the world go by.

My stop comes sooner than I had hoped and also seems to take forever. Luckily I have kept the carriage to myself so I can fumble with the window and the door handle without making a plum of myself and I manage to get off with my case just as the conductor is whistling for the train to continue to Swansea.

I could change clothes here. In the latrines. But I would have to go into the gents and then come out as a girl. I really don't want to do that. Also it is easier to walk in this get up. Stopping outside the station, I check my map with freezing fingers. My breath comes out as if I am a steam train myself. There is plenty of light left in the day as I set off early.

Getting my bearings, I head in what I hope is the right direction, wishing I had enough lolly to pay for some transport other than my feet. I also don't have any income to support my mother once I have rescued her. I've weighed up the options and I'm hoping there will be a manor house of some sort where I can get work to keep us. If not, I have my maid's outfit in my case and will have to steal to get us board and lodging until I can find something suitable. I imagine us in our own cottage together one day. It isn't too much to ask, is it?

I have been walking forever. My boots are too tight and worn at the sole and I'm tired and hungry. It's colder out here in the open country and my fingers are blue at the tips and my nose is frozen. I'm very lucky – Dylan gave me some cake for the journey. They have been taking such good care of me. Since the ship set sail, the mudlarks have taken it in turns to house me where they can and suggested sleeping places where they can't. I will repay them all for their kindness one day.

I stop for a moment, balancing my case on a grass verge and taking out the slab of cake. Gnawing on it ravenously, I check the map again. Churches are a good landmark to go by as their spires are so easy to spot and I can place myself on the map thanks to one I can see fairly easily and one that's far away. If my calculations are correct that distant spire is where I'm headed. I'm nearly there. This realisation and the cake give me new energy.

'There you go, sweet pea,' I say to a little hopping blackbird, throwing it some crumbs. He orange-beady-eyes me and decides that I have gone completely loopy. Agreeing, I grab up my case and run for a bit then slow when I am out of puff.

I think about my plan, such as it is. I will get into the asylum with my maid's costume. I presume they have maids. I will find my mother's room. I try to block out thoughts of what state she may be in. She will recognise me. I hope. I have forged a letter from Sid. I have delivered so many messages from him I know his signature by heart. It isn't perfect but it will pass. Unless he has warned them that someone has been rifling through his secret drawer. Unless...

The church is surrounded by a low wall and I clamber over it rather than going through the lych-gate at the front. There doesn't seem to be a soul about but it's better to be safe than sorry. I walk its perimeter. Ducking behind gravestones. Reading the carvings on some, righting the flowers on others, stalling for time. I'm scared. Dead scared.

'Pull yourself together, Nansi, you giant namby-pamby.' Scolding myself works a bit so I continue. 'Come on you dunderhead. You ninny. You halfwit.'

As I reach the back of the church, I realise just how close I am. There, just beyond the churchyard, is a collection of buildings that can be nothing other than the asylum. I am elated to have found the right place but dismayed to see there is more than one building. I hadn't anticipated that. I scan the many windows hoping for a glimpse of a woman with gleaming red hair. No such luck.

There is no turning back. I check the graveyard for any visitors then hide behind a yew tree and open my bag. There is the maid's costume I so hated before. How strange that something which has been a shackle will now help to set me free. I hope.

I strip out of the boys' clothes and dress as nimbly as possible so that I won't freeze to death. The dress material is so much thinner than the trousers and shirt. I should have kept them on beneath. It's too late now as I've thrown then down on the damp ground in my haste and they're wet. Hopefully some passing needy person will find them. I take a deep breath and put on the cloak that I have brought to put over my mother. I face the asylum full on. This is it.

13

I don't have Bee's gift for invisibility but I have had to practise going unnoticed. Heck, my whole life at the theatre has been largely being unnoticed, so I should be good at it by now. I climb over quite a high wall to get in. Trying to seem as if I'm supposed to be here, I look at the different buildings and assess which one my mother might be in. Adrenaline zings through my veins and I think if someone tried to stop me now, I'd knock them down with the sheer energy I have built up around me.

I guess the men and women would be kept separate, as they are at the workhouse. I walk as if I have somewhere specific to go. The cold is on my side, keeping everyone inside. Some male inmates wander about the garden but there are no women to be seen. Typical that even here men have more freedom to come and go as they please.

It should be easy enough to find the kitchens. On cue a delivery boy comes through the main gates and heads around the side of the building on his bicycle. If that's where the tradesman's entrance is, that's where I'm going.

I'm glad I've eaten as the air is thick as soup with the smell of stew as I enter the kitchens.

'What are you staring at?' The cook's face is moon-round custard and poppy red. She squints at me beneath unkempt thorny bush-brows.

'I'm delivering something.' I show her the letter I have signed myself.

'Well, be quick about it. Dragging your heels and gawking at everyone.' Her ten chins wobble. 'Who is it for?'

I panic. It's like pins pricking all over my skin. But then I remind myself I am an actress. I've been on stage in front of hundreds of people. 'One of the women.'

I say it with a bored face as if I do this every day of the week.

'Well, you are headed in the wrong direction.' She shakes her head and her chins keep wobbling when she stops. 'New, are you?'

I keep my nerve. 'Not that new.'

'Cheeky little sausage, that's for sure. And scrawny as a rake. Come back for some stew when you've done.' She stirs at it, then ladles some up to her nose to smell it and quickly puts it back. She has a kind face when you stop to look. 'Go on then. Be off with you.'

I don't need telling twice. I change direction and head the way she pointed, going through a door to a large corridor. Women sit on each side on chairs, some sewing or embroidering. Others sit with their hands in their laps and look as if their heads have been emptied of thoughts. A couple of staff glance in my direction but nothing comes of it.

One of the women grabs hold of my skirts.

'What? What do you want?' I'm trembling with fear. At being caught and also that she may be a lunatic.

'You have beautiful eyes.' Her skin is paper thin with blue river veins criss-crossing it.

'Thank you.' I try to wrestle my skirt away from her but her grip is stronger than I thought.

'You have her eyes.'

She has my attention now.

'And her hair. Like flames in the sun. Like fire burning brightly.'

I crouch down in front of her. None of the staff are paying any heed and the other inmates look lost in their own worlds.

'Who are you talking about?'

'She cries a lot, that poor woman. Doesn't want to be here.'

I prise her hands from my dress and hold them both gently but firmly. 'She looks like me? This woman?'

'Such hollow soulful cries.'

'Where is she?'

'She doesn't want to be here. None of us want to be here.'

I grip her hands a little tighter than I should. 'Please tell me where she is. Please. I have to find her. She is my mother.'

The woman looks deep into my eyes. Her fingers are petal soft. She very slowly raises her gaze up. 'They keep her too high to climb down. She tried to escape too many times.'

'Thank you. Thank you.'

One of the nurses is coming towards us. I pretend to be hooking a button on my boot then walk away. I wish I could help this woman. I wish I could help them all.

I keep walking at a steady pace, being careful not to draw any attention to myself. Some of them call out to me and it breaks my heart to keep walking but I have to concentrate.

I come to the main stairwell and see that there is a reception desk with a woman bent to a paper at it. I turn away. If there is a public stairway there will also be one for staff.

Further along, there is. I'm so happy I'm right. I just hope I don't bump into anybody on my way up.

It feels like someone is looking over me, helping me. I take the steps three at a time and I don't meet anyone. The dinner gong sounds a rumbling clang from far below in the heart of the house. That must be why there is no one about. They are all on their way to eat that stinking stew, the poor things. I have to move even more speedily, to get to my mother before they take her for dinner. Perhaps they deliver dinner to her if she is locked in.

The stairs get more and more narrow. At the top I stop for a second to catch my breath then clatter down the corridor, opening doors left and right, one after the other, to empty rooms.

Leaving them wide open, so the cleansing light floods in to chase out the dark. They all seem abandoned. Empty and stark. I'm in the wrong place. I must try all the doors just to be sure. I fling each one open. Something wild has taken me over and I can't be careful anymore.

'Argh.' I can't help myself from yelling in frustration. She is so close. I will try every door in this place until I find her.

'Is there someone there?'

I stop stock still. Someone called out. Or did I imagine it?

'Hullo?'

I definitely heard someone that time. I creep in the direction of the words.

'Hullo? Is there someone there?'

I can pretend to be a maid. I can run. I can defend myself. I can be pretty tough when I want to be and the person sounds scared. They've stopped speaking now. Perhaps they think I've gone. Whoever it is, they are behind the door directly in front of me. Shafts of bright white light line the space behind and I'm sure that someone will be bringing food to this patient soon, so I have to move if I'm going to find out who they are.

I turn the handle but it's locked. I crouch and put my eye to the keyhole. A figure shifts beyond it. With this narrow perspective I can't make out much. I press my eye closer. It's a woman. She is wearing a dress and pacing the room from side to side. Because of the height of the lock I can't see above her waist though.

I have to go in.

Underneath my mob cap I have put hairpins in my hair in case I needed them. I would feel smug if I wasn't so intent on what I was doing. I check that there is no one behind me, but all there is are those undisturbed slats of white light. I can't hear anyone coming up the stairs either. All is good.

My lock-picking skills serve me well and I hear the click as it gives. I'm suddenly unsure, nervous, self-conscious. I don't have time for these feelings. I straighten my hair and turn the doorknob.

My mother is there.

14

'Nansi!'

I rush into my mother's outstretched arms. And she knows me. My biggest fear evaporates in a cloud of dust.

'Mother. I've missed you so much.'

I can hardly get the words out. We stand there, caught somewhere between laughing and sobbing, twirling and cuddling and dancing. And I don't ever want to let go. But I must.

'We need to get out of here.' I look into her beautiful face and try not to ask all the questions inside me. 'We can talk later but for now we need to move.'

'Yes.'

She stares into me with her navy eyes and I see that the years have passed but she is the same. Strong and beautiful. Intelligent. She also looks exhausted and I know that I will have to take the lead.

'Let's go.' I scan the room. 'Do you have anything you need to take with you?'

Her hand goes to her neck as if she has a scarf or something she wants to put on against the chill. 'I don't need anything.' She takes my hand in hers.

I take off the cloak. It's forest green and will act as camouflage once we are outside. If we get outside. I wrap it around her. 'It's cold out there.'

It will hide her vibrant hair if she puts up the hood.

'We need to get going immediately.' I am surprised by how authoritative I sound.

'Let's go.' My mother also sounds strong, though she is so thin and she seems frail.

I feel a new wave of fury towards Sid but I will have to deal with vengeance later. For now there is only escape. 'This way.'

We go to the top of the stairs. I have slipped the forged letter into my boot and I quickly check it is still there. Doing this gives me a second to realise my error.

'My mistake. We are going to take the main stairs. We have to look as if we are meant to be leaving. As if we have permission.'

'Yes. Good thinking.' She beams at me and I see

the face that so dazzled me in my childhood and now dazzles me again.

'Where is it?'

She wrinkles her brow. 'I can't remember how they brought me up here. I've been here so long.'

My heart swells but I cap it quickly. There is no time for anything but action.

'Come on. Let's try this way.' We rush past all the rooms I had searched. We are too high up to jump. We have to go out the way that people would least expect. 'Here.'

A carpeted staircase with oil portraits and landscapes hung at either side. We allow ourselves the tiniest of laughs, but there is so much fear behind it.

'Walk calmly. We have to seem as if we are allowed.'

We both compose our faces into masks of calm and begin. I can hardly breathe and can see my mother's knuckles are white as she clutches at the banister.

There are three floors. We make it down the first flight of steps without meeting anyone. We carry on without speaking.

Halfway down the second flight, a man who

looks like an affable old professor approaches. We try to look normal.

'Good day.' His pince-nez slip from his nose and he pushes them back so he can continue reading as he is walking. He must love reading as much as I do.

We carry on past him. My mother puts a hand to her heart to express worry. I widen my eyes in agreement.

We are on the last set of stairs now and the main entrance is in front of us. I bend over as if to fiddle with my laces and remove the letter, trying not to crush it I am holding it so tight. This is it.

'Walk with purpose,' I say between clenched teeth. 'We need to convince them that I'm here to collect you.'

She straightens up to her full height and arches an eyebrow disdainfully as if she is here to inspect the place. I'm impressed. We walk straight towards the front door, trying desperately not to break into a run.

'Stop right there.' It is a woman with hair tied back so tightly in a bun that it has stretched the skin from her face so I can see every line of her skull.

My mother turns in an almost regal manner. If

I'd never met her I'd swear she was a duchess. Seeing her like that makes the skull woman falter a little, but she resumes her steely glare. 'May I ask what you are doing here please?'

I've rehearsed my part. 'Excuse me, ma'am, but I am Enid Pettigrew, maid to Mrs Howells here. I have orders to collect her and take her home.'

'Orders from who exactly?'

'Mr Sid Sullivan.'

The woman looks suspicious. 'Let me see that.'

The hateful, horrible old sow.

I pass over the papers with a curtsey and stare at my feet which are twitching to run. I spent long enough forging this document. It is exactly Sid's writing. It has the emblem of the theatre at the top of the page. Whole hours pass in seconds.

The woman sniffs in a piggish way. 'Well, I suppose I must let you go. If that's Mr Sullivan's will. But I don't understand why he couldn't come here himself?'

'He is on stage this evening. He can't let his public down now, can he?' I'm quaking but I still manage to appear calm.

'I suppose not. Though it seems unusual. Perhaps I should send a messenger to check.'

'Please go ahead. I'm certain that your ignoring his orders will put him in a delightful mood.' I make as if to leave.

'No. Wait.' She gives me the papers back reluctantly. She glares at my mother. 'Though I should think he would want to keep you here forever with your moaning and caterwauling.'

'I shall miss you too.' That's my mother and I wonder that she doesn't reach out and slap this woman hard.

'Wait a moment.' Skull Face again. 'There is no carriage.'

'I have ordered it to wait at the end of the drive. So that the horses might not be alarmed by the consistent gongs and dinner bells here.' I can't keep the malice out of my tone. This woman has kept my mother prisoner. 'Some of the sights here are enough to scare them.'

I stare hard at Skull Face so that she will know it is her I am talking about and my mother presses her fingers to her lips to hide a smile.

We are winning here. We are putting one over on this old goat.

'Now really, this is most irritating. I was hoping to get her home before dark and the light is failing already.' I yawn. It is over-acting but I can't help but enjoy it.

'Surely you know how irritated Mr Sullivan will be if you don't follow his word to the letter?'

The woman pulls a prim, tight face. 'Good riddance to you.'

I am furious and want to continue this argument but we have to go. I smile at my mother genuinely and then smile at the woman in the most horrible way I can. We have beaten the evil trout. My mother remains composed. Now I know where I got my acting talent.

The light as we step into the outside world has turned pewter.

'Well done.'

'You were glorious.' She stumbles a little with fatigue then rights herself and struts away from that dreaded building.

I glance back over my shoulder and see that Skull Face is watching after us. We are heading for the main gate and I know it is taking everything in both of us not to break into a run.

'Not far to freedom now.' I'll get us lodgings for the night in Bridgend and then we can make a plan. Everything is possible. We are almost at the gate.

A carriage is approaching. It's fine. Of course there will be people in and out of here to see relatives. Perhaps it is someone who works here arriving or another delivery. It comes through the main gate at a roaring speed, the horses snorting white trails of breath, the driver cracking sharply with a whip. We scurry to the side of the lane. It clatters past and then the driver gives a devilish shriek and the horses come to an abrupt halt. Even now I am reasoning that it could be anybody. Even now I am hoping.

And then the driver hops down and I know that the worst thing possible has happened. It is Sid.

15

'I knew it.' Sid's face is filled with hate.

We are frozen to the spot. I know I can outrun him but my mother is weak from being locked away for so long.

'Nansi.' His eyes are demonic.

'Yes. It's me. I survived you. I will always survive you.' I spit the words at him hoping to scar him with every single syllable.

'And you, dear sister. Where exactly do you think you are going?'

I look around us as if a third party has appeared. My mother's face is alabaster white. I look back at Sid. He is talking to my mother. He is calling her his sister.

Quaking in my boots, I challenge him. 'What?'

His rage turns to mocking in a split second. 'Oh, so you don't know everything then, Madame Detective?'

I stand my ground though my legs are jelly.

'Did you think I wouldn't know someone had been rootling around in my office?' He pretends at disbelief. 'An unlocked drawer. Classic mistake. And then a few questions here and there and a little persuasion. Bee sends her good wishes by the way.'

I hurl myself at him, but my mother holds me back. She is stronger than I thought.

'Quite the little cat, aren't we, Nansi? Just like my darling sister always was.'

'What are you talking about?' I break free of my mother's arms then face them both. 'What is he talking about?'

The anger is bubbling up inside me so violently. I am shaking all over. Sid laughs his most spiteful laugh.

'Not had a chance to tell her you're my sister yet, then?'

I stagger.

'You didn't know?' My mother's cloak catches on the wind like a bird's feather. A screech owl calls in the distance. Stars begin to prick the sky as the light is leached from the world.

'He's your brother?'

'Nansi has memory loss, you see. The poor little thing. Such a shame. And so very convenient. Now get in the carriage and you too, darling sister. This is exceedingly tiresome and I'm peckish.'

I stare at my mother with disbelief. How can we be part of him? The same family?

'Come on. Time is short and I do have a part to perform tonight. I'm sure I can get you a room next to your mother's in there, Nansi.'

He smirks and I see Skull Face has appeared on the porch and is watching us keenly. As I look two men come up to join her and she points at us.

I make my eyes downcast and pretend to be broken. He turns to open the passenger door to the carriage for us and I take the chance.

'Run.' I grab my mother's hand and we race for our lives out through the main gate and along the lane.

I hear Sid curse behind us, then holler to the people from the asylum to help. Horses bray and I know that he is going to try to catch us in the carriage.

'We need to get off the road.' I tug my mother towards a thicket and we stumble through the cold, marshy bog, wrenching our ankles and knees in potholes, but keeping on until we are concealed by the thorns. I peer back, just in time to see Sid yanking at the reins and the horses losing their footing.

The carriage slides as if on ice and then tips with an enormous crunch, landing on its side, a wheel spinning pointlessly in the air.

We don't speak. We just watch. Trying to catch our breath. There is no movement from the cabin. The horses have fallen too and are letting out horrifying shrieks of pain. I need to go and free them. I recognise the sound of agony too well.

I am about to tell my mother to wait while I go, when the carriage door flings upwards straight to the sky. Sid hauls himself up with swearing and curses. He is bleeding from cuts on his face and his left arm hangs at the wrong angle from his shoulder. He throws his head back and roars at the sky, scaring up a murder of crows to shock the air with their cries.

If he catches us there will be no more chances.

'I can't run any further, Nansi. I'm so tired.'

'We have to keep going. We have got to find somewhere to hide.'

She grimaces then sets her face in determination. 'Which way?'

'Let's go into the wood. We have more chance of losing him in there.'

'Yes. Good. I'm very proud of you, Nansi.'

A feeling wells up inside me that I haven't felt in a long time but I have to contain it. If I am distracted for a second, that gives Sid a chance to find us.

I peer through the bushes again. I can't see him. Where is he? He wouldn't give in that easily. I can't see him lying injured somewhere. He isn't screeching either.

Skull Face and the men rush to the carriage in consternation. We have to move.

'Mother, we need to...'

I turn. To my horror Sid is holding a knife to her throat.

'Did you really think you could beat me, Nansi?' His good arm pulls the knife even closer to her skin. 'After all these years?'

His pupils glitter. He is insane and there is no reasoning with him. He could have called out for Skull Face and the others, but his arrogance has bought us time.

'What do you want from us?' I'm asking the question to get more time to think. I can't go for the knife – he would slice my mother open. I look at his damaged arm hanging limp.

'I want what's rightfully mine!' He sprays spittle like bullets. 'Why should she have everything? She could never put a foot wrong, always the favourite one. My mother loved her so much. Always gave her everything. And then you came along. Blessed little grandchild and I may as well have not been born. I only put my mother in the asylum to scare her. She was never meant to die.'

He lets the knife move away from my mother's throat a little.

'And then when she did, Father blamed me for everything. He signed it all over to *her*. The house. The money. Everything.'

There's no way he will fall for a 'What's that?' over his shoulder trick. I don't know what to do. If I run at him, he will hurt my mother.

She looks at me and I know to be ready for something, because we can still communicate without words. She bites down hard on Sid's hand. The pain shocks him into letting go his grip. I pull her and we are running again deep into the woods.

Branches try to hold us back, we trip on roots and ground ivy, the light is a thick murky green. Sid is close behind, baying and yowling like a slavering dog. But we are together.

If I trip, my mother helps me up. If she falls, I grab her before she hits the floor. We can't let him catch us.

We run into a clearing and have to cling on to each other not to fall straight over the edge of a steep bank. A torrential river runs through it. Its howling waters fill the air and boom up to the sky. It soaks us as it splashes against rocks. My mother wears a diadem of droplets.

I search around frantically for another way. A bridge, stepping stones, a path around this bubbling cauldron. There is no way but through.

'We have to swim.'

'I can't. I don't know how.' She is petrified. I hold her shoulders with as much strength as I can manage.

'I will help you.' I sound so much more confident than I feel. This river may be too much for me, let alone carrying the weight of someone else. I don't know if I can make it.

'Don't be ridiculous, Nansi.' Sid has caught up

with us. He doesn't need to rush any more. There's nowhere for us to go.

'Why would you do this to us, you evil, horrible…' I can't think of words heinous enough.

I stand in front of my mother.

'Me evil? Me?' He is incredulous. 'When she got everything? I'm the one to blame?'

My mother leans past me. 'They tried to help you. They kept giving you money and you kept gambling it away.'

'We can't all be as perfect as you.' He is burning with a hatred that could set light to the trees. He still holds the knife but at some point it must have slipped because his hand drips blood.

'They would have supported you, if you'd only stopped.'

'They wrote me out of their will because of you.'

'No, Sid. They wrote you out because of *you*. Until you changed your ways.'

'They would have left me to die at the hands of debt collectors, of cut-throats, of killers.'

'No, they wouldn't.' My mother's pleading is causing her so much pain. 'They just wanted you to promise to try to live a better life. That's all they wanted.'

His jugular vein pulses so hard I'm afraid it will split his neck open. I've seen Sid angry before but this is something different.

'A better life?' He throws his head back and laughs at the lavender moon. 'The life of a saint or worse still, a teacher like you.'

'There is nothing wrong in working hard.'

'I can't think of anything more drab.'

I've been quiet long enough. 'I can't think of anything more delightful.'

'Shut it, Nansi. All the women in my family talk too much. And I deal with them all.'

He makes a swipe for me and I step back, almost toppling my mother over the edge. I stand beside her and put my arm about her waist for support.

'Lucky for me that my father's gone doolally because he can't find his daughter or his granddaughter. Boo-hoo. I will be put in charge of everything when he dies. If only he would get on with it, eh? Because now there will be no one else to inherit. My darling mother popped her clogs and I've had enough of trying to be kind to you two.'

I can't believe I was ever taken in by this

charlatan. Perhaps he does have a talent for acting after all. Perhaps I am too quick to trust. He is so, so close to us. I could reach him if I stretched out my fingertips.

'And now I'm going to have it all. The house. The money. The fame. Everything. That'll teach you to cross me. I will get my own way.'

I say, 'You really are pathetic.'

There is nothing he hates more than being called pathetic. He told me once when he was drunk that his mother called him this. Only I would know how much it would hurt him. It shows how close we once were. I'm pleased to have gotten under his skin. And then immediately I'm not. I'm just sick of it all.

'We've survived you once and we will do it again.'

I allow myself one moment of preparation and then I jump, into the river, pulling my mother with me.

The cold is beyond anything I have ever known. The weight of two bodies is too much. My mother is splashing so hard she is going to drown us both. I lose the sky and then come bubbling up, gasping and screaming.

'Trust me.' I hold her fast. 'Stop fighting. You have to trust me.'

I kick out hard. Choking against the water filling my lungs. Holding my mother's head above the surface, I concentrate on moving backwards, using the current to help me to the far side, not trying to fight against it. The water is always stronger. If you try to work against it, it will win.

Eventually, after what feels like days of intense pain, I feel the land behind me. I tip my mother on to it and lie helpless as she crawls up the muddy bank towards safety. I am spent. There is no energy left in my body. I cling to the mud of the bank with my fingers and feel the water laughing in my ears. It wants to drag me away.

I laugh back and using every ounce of grit and determination begin my sliding crawl up the bank. My mother is at the top. She is being sick. I crawl towards her on my hands and knees and then we hold each other, shivering and freezing, but laughing beneath it all.

'Nansi.' It's Sid. He is screaming at me from the other side of the bank and his teeth are bared like a fox.

I can't answer. I won't waste the energy on saying a single thing.

'You will not escape me, Nansi.'

He is livid. It's like watching something from a dream. My lack of response is pushing him to even further rage and I'm glad of it. I watch him run this way and that and feel nothing.

'I will not let you escape me.' He plunges straight into the river.

I'm not laughing now. There is a strange gurgling noise in my throat.

The world turns.

He starts to struggle. Going under, and again.

I might be able to save him. I might be strong enough to dive in after him and bring him back to land.

I watch him disappear.

16

The light rises over Cardiff, just the same as any other dawn. Gulls soar in brilliant white over the town. The sun has been newly born and I am another Nansi. I am Nansi. I'm not Ruby. I'm not Tilly. I am me.

We are on our way home in a carriage and though we are both exhausted we can't go straight there because I have to pick up Bee first. I won't leave her alone another second.

It seems so strange to use the word 'home'. I roll it around inside my mouth like a succulent purple plum. In spite of being so terribly tired, we have talked most of the way, but now Mother has fallen into a deep and peaceful sleep and I am marvelling at everything alone.

No wonder Sid didn't want me to steal from the house he told Bee to rob from. My grandfather had promised to call the police if he so much as set eyes on him. Sid had told my grandfather he was helping my grandmother with doctors and experts when she got melancholia. She died almost as soon as he put her in that place. I can't imagine the pain she went through. That we all went through because of Sid.

Things will be better now. I think of the home we are going to. No wonder it was so comforting and familiar and I felt as if I knew it all so well. As my mother described her home to me, I realised that it was the house with the casket hidden in the wall. It had felt familiar, like something from a story. When we ran from Sid and fell into the river that awful day, I forgot everything, but the memory of it must have stirred somewhere far, far inside.

The carriage pulls up outside the Empire and my mother half wakes as it jolts. I pat her hand. 'Wait here. I won't be long. I promise.'

The foyer of the theatre smells different today. The excitement I used to feel at being a part of this world is gone. The walls are stained brown with tobacco and the posters curl at the edges. There is hardly anyone around.

Last night, we were found in the woods by a local poacher. He took us in, fed us vegetable broth, and kept us warm and safe till morning. We travelled before the light woke. My mother wanted to be as far as possible from that place she had been kept in for so long. Not many people travel by carriage in the dark, it's not safe, but the poacher, having heard our story in a mixture of disbelief, disgust and eventual delight, agreed to take us to a friend of his who would bring us to Cardiff. My mother tried to press payment on him in an I.O.U. but he was having none of it. He said he seeks redemption daily for his own criminal acts and this would buy him a week or even two of feeling good about himself.

I hear footsteps approaching and hide in the shadows. I'm almost as good at it as Bee. I don't want to see anyone – I'm too wrung out for explanations.

I pass by my old room. The door is flung open and the flowers I loved have been tipped over and died.

Bee is a little further down. I worry at what state she might be in. I know I had no choice but to leave her, but I hope she has coped alone. I push the door open. She's lying in bed. She is so still. My heart pounds in my chest like a hammer and I'm almost too afraid to go over to her. What if she got too ill while I was away? What if she died? As I have this terrible thought, she pulls her blanket up closer to her chin. She is asleep. I tiptoe over to her and stroke her hair. She wakes and leaps up with an excited squeal.

'Nansi! It's you. You came back.' The talking sets off her cough and when it stops her breathing is laboured.

'It's all right, Bee. It's all right.' I hold her tight. 'I'm going to take you home with me now. We'll get a proper doctor to see you. We are going to live together. I have someone to introduce you to.'

'You found her?' Her eyes fill with hope.

'I found her. And she is so looking forward to meeting you.'

Bee goes to pick up her few clothes. They are so scratty and patched. I don't want to offend her but I put my hand on hers and stop her. 'We are starting all over afresh.'

She looks around the room. 'You mean I'll have to give up all of this?'

'Yes. I know it will be a wrench of sorts but...'

She interrupts me with a wink. 'Well, thank goodness for that.'

We laugh then, like sisters.

'I mean I'll miss the crate for a bed.' We are hysterical with giggles even though Bee is coughing on and off. 'And the stench that stinks the place out.'

I am laughing so hard I'm snorting.

'But apart from that I think I'll manage.'

When we get outside, I take a lingering look at the place which was my home for so long. Then I turn my back on it and breathe in a new city.

'Bee, this is my mother. Mother, this is Bee.'

They shake hands formally then my mother gives Bee an enormous hug.

'Now, Nansi. We must get this sorted once and for all. You must not call me Mother. It's far too staid. Why don't you call me Ma?'

'Ma.' I try it out. 'I like it.

'And Bee. I absolutely insist that you call me Ma from now on too. Otherwise I'm afraid the deal is broken and you can't come and live with us.'

I blink hard. I have told my mother Bee is an orphan. She is trying to make her feel part of the family.

'Go on Bee. Try it.'

'Ma.' Bee says the word so quietly that we can hardly hear her.

'What was that?' I put my hand behind my ear and pretend I have gone deaf.

'I said, Ma,' she repeats it louder.

'Nope. Still didn't quite catch it.'

'I said MA!'

The three of us burst out laughing and the noise startles the horses.

I look at this all new family of mine and I couldn't be happier if I'd been hailed the leading star of the grandest stage in London.

17

December 1899

We're playing Hide and Seek and it's my turn to seek. It might seem like a childish game for girls our age but when you have been cooped up in the dark for so long, it's great fun. It's difficult to find Bee as she is so good at making herself invisible. I get down on my hands and knees and look under the bed. Of course, she isn't there. No one ever really hides beneath the bed, unless they are a very small child and don't know any better yet.

It's been snowing on and off for the last couple of days and the silvery light makes the china-blue walls glacial. I try the wardrobe, pushing aside all the wonderful new clothes my mother has had made for me. Iris-blue velvet dresses and deep magenta silks. She isn't there either.

I go to the window and look out. We scraped

together enough powdery snow to create a snowchild. It smiles up at me with its coal mouth. The glass is cold and my breath makes circles of condensation. I draw the shape of hearts in them then wipe them off with my fingertips. There's no sign of Bee out there. She must be downstairs.

'Ma'am.' One of the maids, Dilly, is carrying some fresh linen up the stairs as I go down.

'Please call me Nansi.'

'Sorry Ma'am, I mean Nansi. It's force of habit.'

'I can't bear all that fuddy-duddy stuff. Now, very importantly, have you seen Bee anywhere?'

She grins in a way that tells me she has.

I laugh. 'Thank you.'

The Christmas tree at the bottom of the stairs is huge and lit by candles. It smells of a mixture of pine needles, cinnamon sticks and the oranges which Cook dried out in the oven so we could make them into stained-glass window decorations.

Bee isn't in the parlour. Ma is sitting at the table writing in her journal, curls of steam rising up from her teacup. She has Earl Grey with a squeeze of lemon. I tried it so that I could be like her but it's like drinking perfume. She is thinking of writing our story into a great novel which will travel the world. She will have a pseudonym of course and the characters will have different names. But it will be our story nonetheless. It starts when my father dies from cholera, which he really did. He was a teacher at the Cardiff University. Pernicious Sid made up all the nasty things he told me about him. He wasn't running after us that day. It was Sid we were running away from. I'd presumed that Sid was just passing and took me in out of the kindness of his heart. How naïve I was.

The thought of Sid is a dark shadow in the room. I still have nightmares about him. I still see him being dragged away by the river. The Empire Theatre burned down on October 31, 1899. Set alight by a fault with the gas-lighting the newspapers say. How apt that it would happen on Halloween. I like reading the paper, knowing about current affairs now that we are at the beginning of a new century and things are changing. I wonder if that was really the cause of the fire.

In another newspaper, a few days later, there was an announcement of a wedding: Mr Gideon

Gilbert and Miss Lavender Day. The woman's face in the photograph is covered by a veil, and the man sports a finely waxed moustache, curled up at the edges, and thin metal-rimmed reading glasses. I have studied that photograph over and over. I can't be sure but it looks so much like Sid. They were about to take the ship across the ocean to America to make Moving Pictures.

I can't be sure. And yet, deep down inside I am. I hope that his life works out well in America. That he is not the shadow behind the trees. That ripple in the curtains of my room which makes the gaslight flicker. The ghosts of my past will always be with me.

At Ma's neck is the locket we have retrieved from the pawnbrokers. It was my hair inside it. The casket was hers. She had hidden some money there when Sid started stealing from her and her parents. Sid forced her to tell him where it was eventually, though she kept it to herself for years. I suppose his desperation for money as the Empire was failing made him finally force it out of her. The book of Andersen's Tales was mine, my mother used to read it to me when I was very young. As my memory comes back in fragments,

I realised I was reading it in her voice inside my head the whole time we were apart.

Bee isn't in the drawing room either though my grandfather is. He has a book face down in his lap and is having a nap in front of the fire. Mine and Bee's stockings hang at either end of the mantelpiece, waiting to be filled tonight. I take a candied fruit from a silver tray and pop it in my mouth. I know where she'll be.

The library is my favourite place in the whole wide world. I could stay in there for eternity. Sometimes we choose books that are on the highest shelf just so that we can slide the ladder across on its castors to get to them. Sometimes we make big piles of books on the reading table and spend hours poring over the history of the world or losing ourselves in magical lands. At the moment I am scaring myself silly with a novel called *Frankenstein – the Modern Prometheus*. It's a humdinger of a story which chills me to the bone and I love it. Ma says that everyone should read Mary Shelley because she is a modern woman and doesn't let men tell her how to live her life. She says that children's books are often made kinder so that we won't be scared. I lend her my copy of Grimm's Tales and tell her to read about Cinderella's sisters.

I spin the globe that stands on its brass axle as I look about me. There, behind the heavy velvet drapes, are two feet sticking out. I hum as if I haven't spotted her and then at the last moment spring towards the curtains and scare her out of her hiding place.

'Found you.'

Bee squeals then pummels me. I run around the library then climb a ladder so that she can't reach me. She slides the ladder along its rail and I laugh even harder.

The bell clangs in the hall. 'I'll get it, Dilly.'

Dilly stops in her tracks and lets us rush past her. The postman brings cards and Ma has made us write one to each other and post it for fun.

Sure enough, amongst lots of cards and letters addressed to Ma and Granddad there is one for me and one for Bee.

'To Nansi Sullivan.' I read my real name aloud. All those years I thought I was called Howells. I would have been able to find my family if Sid had let me know my real name. I unstick the envelope, then I bite down hard on my fingers not to say anything. Bee has drawn a likeness of the two of us and written 'Sisters at Christmas' as a title. Inside she has written a lovely note and I am so proud of her handwriting.

'It's beautiful.' I can hardly trust myself to speak. 'Go on. You open yours.'

She does and then makes a face of such astonishment that I am laughing again. I've also drawn a picture of us together with the title 'The Christmas Sisters'.

'Great minds think alike.'

She nods.

Later Ma asks me to read to everyone. Standing in front of the fireplace with my family around me I realise that this is the only audience I will ever need. I am the star of my own life.

I clear my throat then read. 'Marley was dead to begin with…'

I replace the name Marley with Nansi in my head.

Nansi was dead to begin with but now she is alive.

Acknowledgements

Cast

Editor, wonderful lady, patient saint, advisor, maker of laughter, friend – Janet Thomas

Super Agent, buddy, swims with sharks, wrestles bears, likes books, hero – Ben Illis

Box office, marketing, magician's assistants – Penny Thomas, Megan Farr

Spinner of gold, cover creator, perfect with pictures – Anne Glenn

Victorian theatre enthusiast, mentor, alchemist of history, gentleman – Dr Michael Read

Weaver of words, teacher, believer, touches others with magic – Professor Stevie Davies, author

Authors, cheerleaders, spotlights through chaos – Rhian Ivory, Lu Hersey, Sharon Marie Jones

Stagehands, sound technicians, fans at stage door – Mum and Dad

Villain, partner in crime, chef, star – Guy Manning

Daily Agony Aunt, bezzie, reality checker – Joanna Suvarna

Chorus, mostly ginger, all lovely – The Howe family

Chief *cwtch*-er, confidante, dance instructor – Watson Jones, dog

City which I loves (sic), beautiful, interesting, vibrant – Cardiff

The author wishes to acknowledge the award of a **Literature Wales Writer's Bursary supported by the National Lottery through Arts Council of Wales** for the purpose of completing this novel.

Also from Eloise Williams

'I loved this contemporary adventure of witches, curses, identity and belonging, from Wales' Children's Laureate.'
Fiona Noble, *The Bookseller*

'I LOVED Wilde! A wonderful, witchy tale of one girl's struggle to fit in.' Lisa Thompson.

'Full of courage and kindness' Amy Wilson

www.fireflypress.co.uk

Also from Eloise Williams

ELOISE WILLIAMS

SEAGLASS

'A wonderfully atmospheric ghost story' *Claire Fayers*

'She will come for you.' A salty, windswept MG
ghost story set on the west Wales coast

'wonderfully gripping, it dazzles like sea glass itself'
Scott Evans, #PrimarySchoolBookClub

'A wonderfully atmospheric ghost story' Claire Fayers

www.fireflypress.co.uk

Also from Eloise Williams

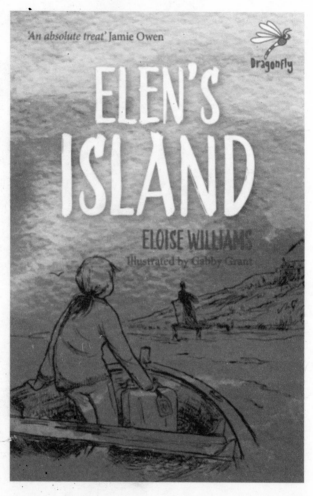

When Elen is sent to stay for the summer with her gran on a tiny island, she's FURIOUS. Gran tells her to explore. But all Elen finds are mysteries...

'Wildly imaginative, funny and poignant ... You'll fall in love with the feisty Elen, her phenomenal gran and a magical island.' Stevie Davies

www.fireflypress.co.uk